THE WILLOUGHBY SPIT
Wonder

THE WILLOUGHBY SPIT
Wonder

Jonathon Scott Fuqua

CANDLEWICK PRESS
CAMBRIDGE, MASSACHUSETTS

Copyright © 2004 by Jonathon Scott Fuqua

First edition 2004

Library of Congress Cataloging-in-Publication Data

Fuqua, Jonathan Scott.
The Willoughby Spit wonder / Jonathan Scott Fuqua. — 1st ed. 2004
p. cm.
Summary: In 1950s Norfolk, Virginia, as Carter and his sister watch their dying father struggle to remain cheerful, Carter decides to emulate Prince Namor, comic superhero, in order to inspire his father to stay alive.
ISBN 0-7636-1776-8
[1. Sick — Fiction. 2. Heroes — Fiction.
3. Fathers and sons — Fiction. 4. Brothers and sisters — Fiction.
5. Norfolk (Va.) — History — 20th century — Fiction.] I. Title.
PZ7.F96627Wi 2004
[Fic] — dc21   2002041141

2 4 6 8 10 9 7 5 3 1

Printed in the United States of America

This book was typeset in Giovanni Book.

Candlewick Press
2067 Massachusetts Avenue
Cambridge, Massachusetts 02140

visit us at www.candlewick.com

To Mom (and my family)

Chapter
ONE

Carter rushed along the shore, through the warm breeze, his white T-shirt whipping against him. Over the water, a seagull hovered like a dirty white puppet, and he imagined himself soaring past it. He jumped, throwing one arm out in front of him and curling the other in a fist at his side. He didn't take off. He ran faster, leaping again and again the same way, until, out of breath, he quit.

Panting, he glanced toward where his sister, Minnie, sat by the dunes with their friend Sylvia. Behind them, the houses seemed to hover, since they were built on stilts that allowed waves to wash beneath them during floods and storms. In fact, almost two hundred years before, the skinny stretch of beach that was Willoughby Spit, their home, was formed by a hurricane, making it seem like it could one day just as easily disappear.

"What're you doing, Carter?" his sister called to him as he walked up.

"Wishing I could fly like Prince Namor."

Minnie rolled her eyes.

Sylvia smiled faintly.

"I know it won't happen. It's just, I like trying."

"Then go on and do it some more. We're talking."

"About what?"

"None of your business."

"Have Mom and Dad gotten back yet?"

"Nope."

Carter stared north along the beach toward the great body of water that was Hampton Roads, which his parents had to cross on a ferryboat to get home from the army veterans' hospital. He imagined their second-rate Henry J automobile swaying on the deck of the ferry and them talking inside it. His mother never got animated anymore, but his father made up for her. He was tall and fun and could cast a fishing rod a half mile or so. During the war, he'd been so strong he'd boxed and been good at it. Carter figured he might be again, even though he was supposed to be dying from something nobody would tell him the name of.

"You know what, Minnie? If I was like Namor, I'd fly clear past Europe and all the way to India. I'd live on the bottom of the Indian Ocean, where animals don't know anything. I'd make friends with the big sharks, and we'd hunt all day and not even think."

"You're being stupid."

"So?" he shot back, watching Sylvia. At the end of school and the start of summer, he'd started liking the way she talked and looked and even how her ankles fit into her socks. He looked over his shoulder and along the shore, where white-tipped waves rushed in at an angle and curled against the beach like a zipper bringing separate sides of a coat together.

He said, "Bye, y'all," and rushed off, zigzagging

and kicking up sand before he got going straight and ran for the dark green Chesapeake Bay, which he hit at full speed, tripping over a small wave and falling headfirst into a larger one.

Underwater, sounds were softer. Holding his breath, Carter listened to the gentle wash of the surf. It was comfortable, like being tucked deep in the cool sheets of a soft bed, except in a bed there wasn't the threat of getting swiped by a passing stinging nettle.

Carter let out some bubbles and wished he could breathe both water and air like Prince Namor, the Sub-Mariner, who was his favorite superhero from the comic books his father had brought home after the war. But he couldn't.

Rising to the surface, Carter opened his eyes to find himself looking straight at a huge gray navy plane flying low with a sputtering engine and two of four propellers already stopped. As big as an island and barely moving, it seemed like it should fall straight to the ground and explode in a fireball, like the alien spacecraft on a movie poster he liked.

Scared, Carter waved his skinny arms and yelled, "Go on! Go on and go!"

The two engines roared louder, and the plane swept overhead, so near he thought he could hit it with a clamshell. It seemed to barely squeak over the dunes, the rooftops, and the single-lane highway that ended a quarter mile away at the ferry launch to Hampton.

Carter scurried from the water and raced up to and past where his sister and Sylvia stood atop a sand dune.

"Is it gonna crash-land?" Sylvia asked him.

"I think," he answered. He rushed down two sandy blocks before stopping at Ocean View Avenue. He didn't even notice the burning-hot concrete against his bare feet. A couple of cars flashed by, blocking his view, so he crossed over the road and the streetcar tracks to the far sidewalk and watched the gigantic gray plane struggle past their peninsula and over Willoughby Bay.

With a loud pop that echoed across the water, the third propeller cut off, and the plane lurched like it was falling, like it would never reach the naval base's landing strip on the far shore.

Carter yelled, "Belly flop in the water!" worried that it was going to smash against the sandy bank. "Land in Willoughby Bay!"

A second later, the plane's black shadow appeared just below its black wheels before connecting together as it landed softly on the edge of the runway.

Carter stepped back. It took him a second to feel happy. Then, when it sunk in that the pilots and the plane were safe, he howled and jumped and made a fist. Sure death wasn't so sure. Carter had always guessed that was the case.

Chapter
TWO

That evening Carter hurled a smoothed-down drift-wood stick into a wave and jogged up the beach and past his father, whom he resembled. Both of them had short brown hair that felt like sandpaper, while their cheeks were narrow and their eyes close together, an arrangement that made them appear slightly devious. "So," Carter said, "then it landed. It came right down and touched against the runway. It looked impossible, but it did it."

"Must've been some particularly fine flying to coax that big plane home."

"That's what I thought." Carter smiled at his dad, who took slow steps and sucked hard at his butterscotch candy cane, which he kept in his mouth as a substitute for the Philip Morris Regulars he had stopped smoking a year before.

"Wish I'd done it," said Carter. "Wish I'd brought that plane in for a landing."

Ray Johnston humorously considered his younger child. "If you'd been at the controls, I have no doubt that plane would be sitting at the bottom of Willoughby Bay. Unless you've been training behind my back, Carter, you can't fly."

"If I knew how to fly, I wish I'd've been flying it."

"You'd be a hero."

"Maybe I could pick from any medal I wanted."

"Maybe," Mr. Johnston said, smiling. "Speaking of heroes, guess what I read this morning?"

Carter turned around backward and looked at the two lines he'd been digging through the sand with his feet. "What?"

Mr. Johnston swallowed. "I read that Hindus,

which is a type of religious group in Asia, are upset that Edmund Hillary and Tenzing Norgay climbed all the way to the top of Mount Everest. What do you make of that?"

Carter answered, "They're jealous is all."

"Naw. They consider the mountain a living thing, like a god, and they didn't believe Everest would ever allow a human to walk on the top of its head the way Hillary and Norgay did. I suppose they're just let down it happened."

Carter, who admired the first men to reach the summit of Mount Everest nearly as much as he admired the Sub-Mariner and the Human Torch, snarled. "Guess they're stupid people, huh?"

Mr. Johnston withdrew his butterscotch candy cane and held it between his thumb and index finger like a cigarette. He raised his brows. "Oh, probably not."

Still walking backward, Carter said, "Dad, anybody oughta have figured out how special Edmund Hillary and Tenzing Norgay are."

Mr. Johnston tilted his head upward, toward the sky, where the first few stars looked like tiny pebbles on a blue plate. "Maybe they should've, and maybe not."

To make sure his father wasn't kidding, Carter turned around to check his expression. He appeared serious enough. What stopped Carter, though, was how, in the dusk, his dad resembled a scarecrow more than a person. A chill rumbled down Carter's shoulders and back. He didn't want to see that his father was shrinking, so he cocked his head sideways and counted the number of homes they had to pass before they got to the boardwalk that ran along the edge of Ocean View Amusement Park, with its roller-coaster ride, Ferris wheel, and shopping pavilions crackling with colored lights.

Over the Chesapeake Bay, a high scatter of red clouds caught the last light of the day.

"Carter, did you know, as big a hero as he is now, when he's not climbing, Edmund Hillary's a bee-keeper? That's a fairly regular occupation, huh?"

"A person's got to be brave to do that."

"Maybe." Mr. Johnston laughed.

At the boardwalk, Carter's father walked up the steps, gripping the railing.

Ahead, a neighbor, Mr. Owens, walked slowly in their direction. When he was a few feet away, he stopped. His tie waltzed in the breeze from off the water and his coat collar lifted at the lapels. He was a sixty-something-year-old man who never wore anything but suits, even on the hottest days, even when sweat slithered down his face like lava from out of a volcano. Because his wife couldn't walk so well, Mr. Owens went about in the company of a tiny dog named Papa Bear. "Stretching your legs, Ray?" Mr. Owens asked in a serious, respectful voice.

Carter's father propped himself against the boardwalk's wooden rail. "Love to wander with my kids, especially without any sort of destination."

"How you feeling?"

"Good. Real good. Bet I could last ten rounds with Marciano."

Mr. Owens scratched at his rectangular chin. "Ten rounds with the heavyweight champion of the world?"

"That's what I said."

A grin spread across Mr. Owens's face. He pointed at Carter's father. "Ten rounds of what, sewing?"

Mr. Johnston wiped at the spittle on his lips. "Sewing wouldn't be bad. I wouldn't want to box that man."

Horrified by Mr. Owens's joke, Carter kneeled down and called Papa Bear over. Glancing up, he said, "Mr. Owens, is Papa Bear really a dog?"

"Course he is. He's a purebred, shorthaired Chihuahua."

"He looks like a rat to me."

"Whoa, Carter. You're gonna hurt his feelings."

Carter nodded. "Guess you can hurt my dad's feelings by saying he can't box, and that's fine, but nobody should be mean to Papa Bear."

Behind his brushlike mustache, Mr. Owens grimaced, all the wrinkles in his face getting narrow and dark. He pulled on the thighs of his trousers and squatted down so that he was eye level with Carter. "I was doing what your father was doing. I was horsing around. I wasn't being mean."

Mr. Johnston said, "Carter, I planned for him to do it when I made my comment about Marciano."

"But you could box again if you wanted, couldn't you?"

A raucous look settled across Mr. Johnston's face. "Well, I couldn't box Marciano. He's the world champeen. He'd kill me. He'd've killed me years ago, and these days he'd kill me even worse."

A pang of fear surged through Carter. He rubbed at Papa Bear's smooth, bony head. "But, Dad, I bet you could box."

Mr. Johnston said, "Naw, I couldn't. I'm done, Carter. I'm dying. I'd rather spend the time I got with you and Minnie and your mom. I'd never waste it training."

Carter studied the dog's bulging eyes. "Yeah, okay."

Mr. Owens stood. He pulled on the backside of his belt and tucked the tail part of his shirt in. "Maybe you'll grow up to be a boxer, Carter. You ever think of that?"

Before his son could answer, Mr. Johnston declared, "A boxer! No, Sid. My boy, he wants to be Prince Namor, the Sub-Mariner, when he's older."

Surprised, Mr. Owens said, "Carter, you want to be a prince?"

Carter's father flicked away the rest of his butterscotch candy. "Come on, Sid, Prince Namor's a superhero from the comic books me and half the GIs in the U.S. Army read during the war. Don't tell me you never heard of him. The Human Torch, Captain America, and Prince Namor used to beat the hell out of the Nazis even before we started to."

"Guess I never took to cartoon strips."

Carter said, "Dad gave me all his old copies, plus they just started printing a new comic about them."

Mr. Owens nodded and asked, "So you want to be a hero when you grow up?"

"Mostly I want to be the Sub-Mariner. I want to be other heroes a lot less."

Carter's father reached into his pocket and unraveled a new candy cane from its cellophane wrapper. Tilting his head, he said, "Isn't that the coolest thing, Mr. Owens? He wants to be the Sub-Mariner when he grows up. He wants to fly and breathe underwater. He wants to have superhuman strength. Man, that's all right! That's bigger than boxing. I'm glad he thinks large. See, the kid who doesn't think on a grand scale, I don't want to be around him for too long. Carter, he thinks huge."

"That's the truth," Mr. Owens agreed.

Carter flushed red about his neck. It was true, he did think big. He wanted to be the Sub-Mariner, but God forbid that never happened, his second choice was any sort of superhero, regular hero, FBI agent, or movie star. He wouldn't take anything worse than one of those. So, feeling pretty darn good about himself for thinking so huge, he scratched at Papa Bear enthusiastically before an odd feeling of unease began to gnaw at the edge of his swelled head. "Mr. Owens, when Papa Bear sits like this, he looks more like a dog."

"I'm sure he appreciates hearing that."

Carter's father waved his hands in disagreement. "Now, hold on. I can't allow that sort of lie to go unchallenged. The truth should be told. He never will look like a dog, and that's all there is to it."

"Ray, you're making Papa Bear self-conscious," Mr. Owens declared.

Carter's dad pointed at the Chihuahua. "You got every right to feel self-conscious, Papa Bear. You look funny. You really do."

Chapter
THREE

As soon as the second matinee ended, hundreds of cushioned seats bounced closed and their former occupants swarmed into the lobby and out the front entrance. Kids stampeded from the theater as if the screen were afire and about to bring the building down. Carter, Minnie, Pruitt, and Sylvia were no different.

As they passed through the chrome doors and air-conditioned darkness of the Ward's Corner Theater, the rainforest-like heat of Norfolk sucked the air from their lungs. Most kids jumped into idling, tank-size automobiles, which, as soon as they were loaded, jetted away, but not Carter, Minnie, Pruitt, and Sylvia. Together, they stood in the shadow of the theater marquee. Beside them was a poster for *It Came from Outer Space*, a 3-D alien-invasion thriller like *Invaders from Mars*, which was the first movie they'd seen that day. For some reason, 3-D space movies were extra popular that summer.

"Before we get on the streetcar, I gotta take a piss," Carter told them, hoping that Sylvia would find his rough language attractive.

"God, you're gross," replied Minnie. "You think we want to know that?"

"Dad says it the exact same way."

"He's a grownup," Minnie explained, acting like her brother was an idiot.

Pruitt said, "If my dad ever said *piss*, Mom'd probably hit him with something. She won't even let our family say *bathroom*."

"*Bathroom!*" Sylvia said, confused. "*Bathroom*'s not a bad word."

"I know."

"How do you tell her when you've got to use it, then?"

"I say, 'I need to be excused, please.'"

Carter said, "I've heard him do it that way."

Minnie asked, "What do you tell her when you're traveling in the car?"

"I say the same thing. 'I got to be excused.'"

"What if you feel like you might burst?"

"I say, 'I got to be excused real badly.'"

Sylvia laughed. "All your mom did was replace the word *excused* for the word *bathroom.*"

"I guess."

Carter looked at Sylvia. "Maybe she doesn't like the sound of the word. I'm like that. I don't ever like to say *chunk* or *meat.* They make me sort of sick-feeling, like I might throw up."

Sylvia smiled. "I don't like to say *jellyfish.*"

Pruitt, who was starting to sweat in tiny beads above his upper lip and around the rims of his glasses, said, "I hate to say *flap.* Like in, 'I got a flap of skin hanging off me.'"

Minnie averted her eyes. "Pruitt, you're sick."

"Leave him alone, Minnie," Carter said.

She scowled at her brother. "Fine, I will, but you know what? If you had any brains, you'd've *excused* yourself in the theater. You ever consider that?"

He stared at her. "I forgot is all."

"Guess you don't have any brains."

He stepped out from under the marquee's shadow and into the simmering sunlight. "Least I don't wear a bra."

Pruitt and Sylvia turned to Minnie. "You wear a bra?"

Minnie's eyes grew wide, and her mouth dropped partially open. She peered down past her dress at her scuffed saddle shoes and white socks. "Yeah."

Ashamed at delivering such a low blow, Carter headed off toward the street. "I'm going to use the bathroom at the Esso service station."

When Carter was done, and Sylvia and Pruitt had also *excused* themselves at the Esso, all four stood and waited for the number 68 streetcar to Ocean View Avenue. It took nearly an hour of frying like bacon along Granby Street for one to rumble from downtown Norfolk. Inside, the trolleylike vehicle smelled of smoldering vinyl, as if the seat covers were melting off their springs. At Bay View Boulevard, Pruitt and some other riders got off. Then Sylvia, Minnie, and Carter moved to separate locations to have an open window. Even though the breeze was hot, it was better than nothing.

Sylvia twisted about and hung over the back of her seat. "*Sangaree* was the best movie I've seen all summer," she announced to both Minnie, who was directly behind her, and Carter, who was across the aisle. "Fernando Lamas is so tough and never seems scared."

Carter said, "I thought *Invaders from Mars* was better."

"Bet you don't like anything with a love story in it."

Carter didn't, but he couldn't say that to Sylvia. "I just thought *Sangaree* was sort of a big bore." He glanced over at Minnie, knowing that she felt the same way. They both preferred straightforward adventures to movies sprinkled with dull romance. But she was still mad at him for blabbing her bra secret and wouldn't look back, which caused him to recognize that he'd gone too far. Their parents had warned him not to say anything about his sister's new undergarment. They'd explained how Minnie was embarrassed, which he hadn't really understood. In a second, anyone could see that Minnie was going to look like their mother, curvy, so that boys would whistle and harass her all over Willoughby Spit.

"Minnie," Carter said, "I'm sorry already. You make me say mean things."

"You're a brat," she answered back.

He could be, which only shamed him because Sylvia heard Minnie say it.

The streetcar screeched and bumped over its uneven rails, all the way down past the big Tidewater Drive intersection and onto Ocean View Avenue. It stopped to let most passengers out at the Ocean View Amusement Park, where a colorfully painted, slightly grimy roller-coaster cart roared down a steep track before hurtling around a hairpin curve and curling away from the road. Sylvia waited till the hollers faded away before she slyly leaned over her seat and whispered through the hot air, "Minnie, I can't wait to get a bra. It'll be like I'm an adult. I . . . I actually want one."

Minnie's eyes widened a fraction.

"It's true," Sylvia said.

"But it's embarrassing."

"It's not. It's like you're almost a woman now."

Minnie barely nodded. "You . . . you really think?"

At Fifteenth View Street, they rang the bell and clambered down to the roadway, which looked like it was in the middle of the Sahara Desert and getting swallowed by shifting sand. They'd been the last passengers left onboard, and they thanked the engineer, who waved. At Sylvia's grandmother's car pad, they said goodbye. Sylvia ran up the cinder-block steps and into her grandmother's home on stilts, while Carter and Minnie went up the block to their place alongside the beach.

Carter, who trailed his sister, said, "Minnie, please don't tell on me, okay?"

She didn't look back. "Why shouldn't I?"

He didn't know. "Because."

She turned. "Say, 'I'm a big baby.'"

"You're a big baby." He smiled.

"Say *you* are. 'Carter Johnston is a baby.' Say it five times, or I'll tell."

Carter stopped. He didn't want to call himself a baby. Still, it was better than his mother doing it. That always made him feel small and stupid. "I'm a big baby. I'm a big baby. I'm a big baby. I'm a big baby. I'm a big baby. Okay? I did it."

She smiled. "Now say it one more time."

"No."

"Say it, or I'll tell."

He said, "I'm a big baby, okay?"

"You are," she told him.

When they tumbled into their darkened house, the screen door spanking closed behind them, Minnie yelled, "Mom! Dad! Carter told Pruitt and Sylvia I got a bra after you said for him not to!"

Furious, Carter eyeballed his sister. "You're a liar," he hissed.

From the darkness of the house, their mother emerged, her kind face pale. The curved lenses of her large glasses reflected the windows and the bright light pouring through the doorway behind Carter and Minnie.

Minnie said, "Carter told Pruitt and Sylvia I got a bra."

Mrs. Johnston peered at her son. "We asked you not to do that."

Surprised by her calm response, he said, "I . . . I won't anymore."

She rolled up a sleeve of her white shirt, then pushed back her dry, dyed-blond hair, and banded it tightly with a purple scarf.

Carter said, "Where's Dad?"

Her lips pulled to one side. "Up the street at Willoughby Motors. They're letting him sit in the air-conditioned showroom. After you guys left, he couldn't catch his breath here, not with the heat like it is. He was having a difficult time. He couldn't even catch it out on the beach."

Minnie said, "Is he dying?"

"No."

Carter scraped a foot on the floor. "Can we go see him, then?"

Mrs. Johnston smiled hesitantly, so that deep dimples formed in her cheeks. "I'm right now going to start making a picnic dinner for the four of us to eat in the showroom. Marvin, the manager, said it'd be all right if we come after they close. It might be that your father even sleeps there on the sofa tonight. He needs the air conditioning."

"If he needs it, he should," Carter whispered.

Mrs. Johnston added, "Once he got in that cold air, he improved. When he was finally comfortable and breathing easy, he told me he was going to have to buy a car dealership so that he could sit in it the rest of the summer."

Carter grinned and glanced at Minnie. "He told a joke, Minnie. That means he's okay."

"He always does that."

"He's fine," their mother promised. "It was a frightening morning, but he's fine now."

Minnie said, "You don't look like everything's going to be okay."

"I'm tired is all. I don't have the energy to make a picnic, but I have to. I told him I would."

"Me and Minnie can do it," Carter offered, thinking

that they'd leave out all the food they disliked, like mustard and vegetables. Besides, their father enjoyed ice cream and cookies and beer on his tender throat more than anything else.

"Carter, I'd prefer for you to get his medicine and pajamas for me."

"I don't want to touch his underwear."

"I'll get those," she told him, smiling like in the old days. She turned and wandered into their narrow kitchen. "And don't ever talk about your sister's bra again."

"I won't," he promised.

Chapter
FOUR

Before the intense heat finally broke, Mr. Johnston spent three days and three nights in Willoughby Motors' air-conditioned showroom. When the place was closed for business, he picnicked and played cards with his family and visitors in the back near the sales offices, where he slept on a modern leather couch with chrome legs. A friend who had worked with Ray Johnston at the Norfolk Shipyard was so taken with the new automobiles surrounding them that he slid behind the wheel of each and ended up buying one the next morning. Therefore, Willoughby Motors' generosity didn't go without reward. They made a sale and pretty much won the loyalty of residents up and down Ocean View Avenue. As far as anybody in the area could recollect, they were the only air-conditioned car dealership in the entire country to allow a sick person to cool down in their showroom.

When Mr. Johnston finally returned home, Mrs. Johnston parked him on the back patio, where the concrete was cracked and broken and resembled large, scattered puzzle pieces, which faded into the wiry grass that turned into sand dunes. From his position, he couldn't see over the dunes to the rolling bay, which had tankers and ships moving across it like mountains of riveted metal, but he seemed pleased for the moment, staring into the mesmerizing sky, strewn dramatically with enormous white clouds that had upper and lower levels and drifted in two directions.

Just over the second set of dunes, Minnie and Carter were digging a wide, deep hole with shovels. They had a few unclear ideas as to what they would do with it, but nothing for sure. Finally, Carter stopped and said, "You think we could make it a trap and cover it with sticks so that people will fall in?"

Minnie rolled her eyes. "That's really smart. How much trouble do you think we'd get into?"

"Nobody would know we dug it. We could even charge money to help people get out."

Minnie leaned on her shovel handle. "Anyone can look out their window and see us working. Besides, how many people have walked by, like fifty? They've all seen us. And the people we'd trap would see us when we lower down a ladder for them."

Carter dropped his shovel and leaped into the hole. It was nearly as deep as he was tall. "Wish there were lions around here. If we caught one, we could sell it to a circus."

"Well, there aren't any."

"God, Minnie, if we can't use our hole for something worth it, I'm done digging." He clambered out clumsily, collapsing a portion.

"Just go ahead and fill it back in, why don't you? I might want to use it for something, you know."

"Sorry."

They sat down and stared out beyond the waves to a battleship bristling with big cannons, guns, and radar. Carter said, "The Sub-Mariner used to bend back cannons like those so that they wouldn't fire right. When the stupid Nazis went and tried, the ones he'd bent exploded at the tip."

Minnie muttered, "Carter, the Sub-Mariner didn't used to do anything. He's not real."

"He used to in old stories."

She threw her hands in the air.

"Wish I could fly out there and bend the guns on that ship. You know?" He glanced over at his sister, who seemed to have decided a long time ago that her brother was a total bonehead. "Think about this, Minnie. Namor was the son of a regular man. Namor's mom was Princess Fen of Atlantis. I guess she was stronger than his father, and so she must have lived longer. I thought about it last night. It's kind of like Mom living longer than Dad. You know?"

"Don't talk about Dad dying, okay?"

The situation rattled through Carter's intestines. He hadn't really meant to talk about death at all. What he'd wanted to do was explain how similar things were between Prince Namor and himself. "Okay."

"We're not in comic books."

"I know. But just because we aren't doesn't mean we might not be special or something. We might change one day when we get older and figure out we have superstrength or know how to fly."

"I am older, and we're not special. I already know."

"I don't think you do."

"Carter," she said, "sometimes you make me worry."

"I never make myself worry. You know what? One afternoon, just to prove to you I'm like Namor, I'll swim clear to Hampton. And when I get over there, I'm going to wait for you guys at the Chamberlain Hotel. You know they'd treat me like a movie star. I'd be the Boy Who Swam Across Hampton Roads. They'd probably give me all the Coca-Cola I could drink."

"You'd drown instead. You'd kill yourself."

He looked at her. "Minnie, have you ever wondered if maybe Mom's from Atlantis? We've only seen her parents twice, ever, and her dad looked funny and had to breathe out of that mask. See what I mean? Have you ever thought of that?"

"Grampa Wheatley needs an oxygen mask because he worked in the coal mines."

"Maybe it's not oxygen. Maybe he's breathing water. Minnie, Mom says she's going to work, but maybe she swims out to visit the rest of her family."

"I've seen her at the shoe store."

"Yeah, but it could be her cover and she only works part-time. Maybe she's not allowed to tell us or something. Maybe, so that she could marry Dad, she had to promise she'd never say a word."

"Stop, Carter."

Because he and Minnie'd had fun digging together, he did what she asked, but staring out toward the battleship as it drifted around Willoughby Spit, he thought, *I'm going to surprise everybody*.

Shortly, their father, who'd gotten lonely, walked up and over the dunes, an aluminum yard chair folded and draped over one of his arms. "Whatcha kids up to?" he asked, plopping the chair down and taking a heavy seat on the nylon webbing.

"Digging a hole," Minnie explained. "We stopped, since Carter didn't think we had a good purpose."

Mr. Johnston said, "Let me see. A good purpose? Hey, you could snare a person with it."

"That's what Carter said."

"I like that idea," Mr. Johnston declared, his eyes gleaming playfully. "If you catch somebody, make sure he has some cash with him. We could use some extra spending money."

Carter wondered how they'd check that sort of thing without talking to the person first. Glancing over at his father, he said, "I told her we should charge people to get out. But Minnie always thinks different."

"What did she say?"

"That we'd get in trouble."

Mr. Johnston took a long breath, something that he'd been unable to do a few days before. "She's a smart one, your sister. I guess we ought to take her advice."

Carter mumbled, "Her advice is boring."

Minnie lurched about, cocked an arm, and punched her brother square in the shoulder.

Carter tilted like a boat blown open by a mine. Unlike Carter, Minnie had inherited her father's boxing ability, and when she hit a kid, that kid felt it clear to his spine and back to the impact spot, which rang with pain.

"God, Minnie!" he yelped.

"How can you be an Atlantian if you can't take a hit from a girl?"

Carter said, "Maybe we both got superstrength."

Mr. Johnston unraveled a butterscotch candy cane and put it between his lips. He looked like a movie star puffing on an expensive, golden cigarette. "It's possible that you're both superpowered, sure."

Carter stared. "Dad, shouldn't you say something to her about hitting?"

Mr. Johnston sunk low in his chair and adjusted his sunglasses with both hands, so that the top of the rims touched his curly eyebrows. Out in front of him, the foamy surf rushed up to a line of seaweed and shells that had formed a stripe along the shore. He turned his head. "Minnie, you watch you don't bend your wrist when you hit. You could sprain it."

She said, "Okay, Dad."

Carter had hoped Minnie would get sent to her room or something, because his shoulder felt like it was broken.

"Now that that's done," Mr. Johnston said, "does one of you want to run back to the house and fetch me a beer?"

Minnie appeared uncomfortable. "Mom said not to let you drink any alcohol."

He smirked at her. "What's it going to hurt, Minnie? I mean, I'm dying."

Carter rubbed at his sore shoulder and watched the waves. "Why do you always got to tell us that? It makes everything seem sad."

Mr. Johnston withdrew his candy. "It shouldn't. It's true, and I want you guys to know it, so that when it happens you won't be surprised."

Carter hesitated. "We won't be surprised."

"I know." Mr. Johnston dug a foot into the sand and lifted it. "Maybe . . . maybe I'm also trying to show you how to live. I want to be an example. I always liked living and thought I was pretty good at it."

Minnie told him, "Everybody likes living."

35

"Not everybody."

"Like who?"

"People who are sad don't. In fact, I got a feeling your mother's not enjoying life so much right now, and I want her to. I'm trying real hard to shake her back to normal."

Minnie was silent for a few moments before saying, "Well, Mom told me you shouldn't have any alcohol."

"Explain to me why."

Minnie scratched at a bug bite on her elbow. "Maybe it'll hurt your head."

"My head's on pretty solid today."

Carter offered, "It might burn your throat."

"Throat's fine enough, at least as good as it's been for a few weeks. Plus, cold things are good for it. I want a beer. That's that. I'll drink it and maybe another, and when your mom gets home, we'll attack her and tickle under her arms till she can't stop laughing and seems like herself again."

Carter stood up. He carefully studied his father and wondered. His mother didn't like to be tickled and could get angry at them. He worried that she might, by mistake, hurt his father with her Atlantian strength. "Dad, did Mom really go to work today?"

Mr. Johnston straightened up in his chair. "I think she did."

Carter tried to be sneaky. "You don't think she might've gone to visit her family or something?"

"In Arizona?"

Minnie scoffed. "Like the biggest dope in history, Carter thinks Mom's parents come from Atlantis, the underwater city."

Mr. Johnston bent forward and rubbed his chin. "That's not the dopiest thing I ever heard. I mean, she says she's going to work, but it doesn't look that way when she gets her paycheck. By the look of her earnings, she might not've worked at all."

Carter made a face at his sister. "See, Minnie," he said, and left to get their father a beer.

Chapter
FIVE

After midnight, without fail, warplanes from the naval base sat on the various airstrips and gunned their engines up and down, ready to protect the coast at a moment's notice. Their roar skipped across Willoughby Bay, rising and disappearing with the wind. When Carter couldn't sleep, he would sit up and listen and get nervous if the jets and propellers seemed to go silent for a time. Supposedly, communist spies were everywhere and always looking for a way to destroy America. He'd start to wonder if

Soviet secret agents had sabotaged the U.S. Navy's planes, and thinking that got his imagination rolling in a bad direction. Sometimes, camped beneath the thin shield of his sheets, he'd start to hear Russian bombers rumbling overhead when they weren't there at all.

If the United States and Russia went to war, a nuclear bomb might get dropped on the naval base, so that all of Norfolk would get destroyed. Whenever Carter thought about it, fear rose up in him like a huge tidal wave. Nobody could rescue anybody from an atomic blast. Everybody would die, and he'd never know why except that communists were trying to take over the world.

It was past midnight, and the breeze ruffled Carter's bedroom curtains, making them seem like the fabric of gently gliding ghosts. The enamel white moonlight draped his floor and dresser, and in the distance the sound of Norfolk's warplanes fell back to a low hum. He wasn't listening to them like he usually did, though. Down the hallway, in his parents' bedroom, he could hear someone crying. It wasn't regular, soft tears, either. Someone was sobbing out of control. He stood up, both curious and slightly worried, then lurched out through his door and toward his parents' room.

Alongside the bathroom and before the steps, he hesitated. Leaning against the door frame, he stood for long minutes before he heard his mother's hushed voice weave in and out between his dad's gasps. "Ray, sweetie, that won't ever stop. We love you, Ray, and that won't ever end."

Between tears, his father replied, "Gloria . . . oh, God, I know. I really do."

Horrified, Carter sank to his knees. He'd thought it was his mother crying. His father never even complained. Sometimes, Carter wondered if his dad was even sad that he was dying and leaving them behind.

"Carter."

He looked into his sister's doorway, where she stood in the blue darkness. He wanted to tell her that he didn't know what was happening. "Dad . . . he's so sad."

"He sometimes cries," she whispered, and left her room. She took one of her brother's hands and led him back to the bedroom they both liked best, the one that overlooked the Chesapeake Bay and Hampton Roads. Every year they traded so that neither had to spend an entire childhood in the bad, small bedroom across from the bathroom and steps.

"Why's he doing it?" Carter asked, his bottom lip trembling.

Minnie sat him down on his bed. "He doesn't want to die. I hear him tell Mom."

"He doesn't?" Carter leaned and touched the wrinkles of his cool sheets, and they collapsed flat. Like a thundershower, emotions welled up and out of him. It was as if he'd been keeping a secret and had, by mistake, spilled it to the one person who shouldn't know.

Minnie gave her brother a pillow to cry into, and, after a short while, Carter calmed down and lifted his wet face. "I thought he was happy."

That's when the first tear wormed down Minnie's cheeks. She shook her head in broad sweeps. "Not all the time." She tipped forward and placed her chin on his shoulder. "Don't tell him you heard. I don't ever."

"I won't," Carter promised, one of his ears muffled by his sister's nightgown collar. "I don't want to."

They went to sleep alongside each other, like two sardines stuffed to one side of a rectangular can. They breathed softly, their legs pretzeled, as curtains rustled and warplanes rumbled. Later, in the quiet morning, the sun rose over the bay and speared through the windows, painting Carter's bedroom wall with the hottest blocks of orange light. Normally, the effect, combined with rising heat, woke him instantly, but he was deep in dreams, exhausted.

About nine, Carter wandered downstairs and took a seat at the table with Minnie and their mother. Minnie was munching soup spoon–size bites of Frosted Flakes, and their mom, her blond hair tied up over her head, sipped coffee from a tiny cup with a blue design on the side.

"Thought you might never get up," Mrs. Johnston kidded her boy.

"I never sleep so late."

"You've been going and going all summer. I guess it caught up with you."

Carter felt like he'd been pulverized more than

42

caught. His mind traveled back to the night before, and he recollected his mother speaking softly to his father, reassuring him as well as she could. He thought of the sobs, the sadness, and the wheezing. Carter knew, as he'd known for a long time, that his father needed to feel hopeful about living so that he wouldn't quit and let himself die. But Carter didn't know how to give him hope.

He sneaked a glance at his sister.

Minnie smiled back at him sadly.

A housefly the size of a marble buzzed about the kitchen as Mrs. Johnston prepared a bowl of dry Frosted Flakes for Carter, which was how he liked it. She gave it to him and sat down. "So, I'm taking the day off," she announced. "As soon as your father gets back, the four of us are going to . . . do something. How's that?"

Carter said, "Where's Dad?"

"Off driving."

"For what?"

"He just wanted to drive." She put a hand on the table, seemingly relaxed, so that her presence felt both calm and spontaneous, like in the past. Then the circling fly struck her hard in the temple. Irritated, she brushed at the side of her head. "Lord!"

Minnie laughed. "He hit you right above your ear."

Mrs. Johnston shoved out her chair and stormed over to the cabinet below the sink. After rooting around for a minute, she located the Flit insect spray, which was Carter's favorite insecticide on account of the soldier saluting on the label. She shot rapid-fire at the fly, filling the kitchen with bug-killing mist. The fly landed on a window, and Mrs. Johnston ended its life with two more blasts of Flit. "What would we do without bug spray?" she asked when its legs stopped moving.

Fanning the clouds about her head, Minnie said, "Use a fly swatter?"

"Don't be a smart aleck."

Lost in thought, Carter tilted his bowl and dumped the last dry crumbs down his throat. He dabbed his mouth with a wrist, and an idea suddenly detonated in his skull. It was perfect. "Mom," he said, barely able to contain himself, "can I go swimming?"

"It's so early, sweetie." She sat back down.

"It's not so early. I got up late."

"Digest a little first." She looked at her daughter. "In a few minutes, you mind watching your brother?"

"Yes."

"Well, I know you *do*, but I need you to."

Minnie said, "Thanks a lot, Mom."

"Minnie," Mrs. Johnston said, her eyes suddenly dangerous.

On the beach, the early-morning sun blazed like a bulb without a lampshade. Below it, the water was streaked silver. Carter waded out past the waves and started swimming parallel to the shore. He took a deep breath and went under in an effort to dive like the Sub-Mariner. Stroking the water hard, he brushed against a stinging nettle, which caused his side to burn. Nervous he'd run into more, he floated to the surface and swam freestyle with his head up. Still, with the help of a powerful rip tide, he shot a half mile down the beach in only a few minutes, coming to shore in front of the Ocean View Amusement Park.

"I was fast, huh?" he said, dripping water, his side red where he'd been stung.

Minnie, who had followed him down the beach, didn't dignify her brother with a reply.

Carter stared at the roller coaster, its tracks rising beyond the boardwalk like a mountain of white toothpicks. "Guess I'll swim back now."

"No, you won't. I'm sick of being your personal lifeguard."

"But I got to keep going, Minnie. I'm training."

"Training for what?"

To stall for time, he shook his wet hair and dug at an ear. "To swim better."

She tapped a finger against her cheek. "You think you can cross Hampton Roads, don't you?"

"I could."

"Yeah, well, think it all you want. If I ever see you start, I'll tell Mom and Dad in a second."

He picked up an oyster shell and launched it over the bay. Watching it fly, he wished he'd never mentioned anything about Hampton to her. Especially because, over breakfast, he'd realized that he had to go. His father needed an uplifting event in his life. Even if Prince Namor was a comic-book hero, that didn't mean Atlantis wasn't real and that his mother wasn't from it. In the middle of Hampton Roads, he'd probably turn right into an amphibian. He'd show his dad that getting things was a matter of wanting. If his dad wanted to stay alive as bad as Carter wanted to be like the Sub-Mariner, it could happen.

Silent, he followed Minnie back up the beach.

At home, their mother and father sat on the front steps of their porch looking out over the homes along Lea View Avenue.

"Hey, Dad," Minnie and Carter said a few seconds apart.

Mr. Johnston tilted his head like a concerned dog, then he grinned naughtily. "Either of you want to know what I got this morning?"

Minnie told him, "I guess."

Their father reached stiffly behind the porch railing and pulled out four Radar Raider squirt guns, three of them still in their boxes. He rubbed a hand down the metallic plastic stock that gave the toy a futuristic look. "Nice, huh? We're going to battle each other this afternoon. Mom and Carter against you and me, Minnie. Basically, it's going to be the Americans against the Russians."

Carter rose on his toes. "Who's going to be Russian?"

"Me and Minnie."

"Dad!" Minnie said, clonking up the steps and pulling a squirt gun from its box.

"Okay, then, you and your mom can be the Russians," he said to Carter.

"Come on, Ray," Mrs. Johnston said playfully, nudging her skinny husband's shoulder.

Carter waved a hand. "No way."

Mr. Johnston laughed as if he'd never wept in his entire life. "Well, you and your mom have to take your pick. You want to be the North Koreans instead?"

"Me and Mom can be Atlantians who're battling America over sunken treasure or something." He looked at his mother, who shook her head like she couldn't believe he'd figured out her secret.

"Fair enough, frogman," Mr. Johnston said, and he leveled his Radar Raider and blasted his son in the head.

Mrs. Johnston said, "Oh, Ray, careful you don't hit him in the eye."

"Wish I had. That way he couldn't aim."

"Wish this took real bullets," Minnie said. "I'd shoot Carter right in his tracks."

Carter went up past his sister and got a Radar Raider from its box. "When I get some water for this, Minnie, you're dead."

Chapter
SIX

Early in the evening, as the amusement park's soaring Ferris wheel smoldered radiantly, Minnie and Sylvia raced down the beach from the blunt tip of Willoughby Spit. They paused as they passed over the top of the first set of dunes, marveling at the beautiful and faraway boardwalk, which seemed like a perfectly scaled model lit by Christmas lights. Then they went on, down the back of the dunes and over the next set till they were rushing around the house. Side by side, they sprang up the long front-porch steps, said hello to Mr. and Mrs. Johnston, and let the screen door slam behind them.

"Carter!" Minnie shouted. "Hey, Carter!"

Carter, who was up in his room, draped over his bed and rereading comic books, stopped halfway through turning a page. "Yeah, what?" he hollered back.

"Me and Sylvia found something!"

"What?!" He rolled onto his side and scratched at his bare stomach.

"You got to come see!"

"Tell me what it is!"

"Just come on and we'll show you!"

Mrs. Johnston got up and pressed her nose against the front-door screen. "You two stop yelling back and forth."

Minnie looked at her. "Yes, ma'am. Carter, just come on! Mom doesn't want us yelling!"

Carter closed his comic book and went downstairs. "What is it?"

Sylvia blurted, "A dead shark."

Carter leaned against the back of the couch. "How big?"

"Like six feet."

"That's as big as a grown person!"

Minnie said, "You got to see it."

Carter followed the two girls out the back door, leaving it unhooked and blowing in the breeze. Together, they hurried along the beach. The stormy sky was filled with heavy gray clouds that were smeared purple in places by falling rain. Below those, the open water was peppered with leaping whitecaps and waves taller than them. The three went a quarter mile around the curving tip of land, till they were within sight of the ferry launch's lights and directly across from the city of Hampton. Ahead, along the bubbly water's edge, a crowd of locals had gathered around a large off-white lump. Carter, Minnie, and Sylvia got closer, and Carter spotted one of the shark's pectoral fins sticking up in the air like it was a wing on the Nazi rocket he'd just seen in a Human Torch story.

The three of them slipped through the small crowd and walked around the shark, slowing as they passed the ranks of sharp, white teeth that were exposed by its partway open mouth. Carter stopped and touched the skin alongside its gill slits.

Sylvia said, "What's it feel like?"

"Sandpaper. You got to touch it."

"I don't want to."

Carter ran a finger down the shark's entire body, stopping near its big tail. "Wonder if it's so scratchy because it's dead? Touch it. It's okay."

"Quit trying to force her," Minnie told him.

Carter squeezed the tip of the animal's tail with his fingers. He looked at Mr. Panzer, an old man who lived alongside the ferry launch. "Mr. Panzer, how'd it get here?"

"Coulda washed in from the ocean. Coulda found itself in the bay and got lost and died."

"It's big."

"Seven feet."

"You think it could eat a person?"

"Not in one bite. Still, it could take out a hunk of flesh that'd kill."

Carter peered over a shoulder and across the wide Hampton Roads to the distant Chamberlain Hotel located on the tip of Old Point Comfort. It would soon be his destination. Still, there was so much water in front of him, with only the little island, Fort Wool, between. There had to be more sharks the same size swimming about. But that was okay, he told himself. He'd probably get along with them just fine. Most likely he'd make friends with all sorts of sea creatures. "But . . . Mr. Panzer, it's not from around here, you don't think?"

A lady said, "I've lived here my whole life and never seen a shark that size."

An older kid named Charlie Dane, who was a sophomore at the high school Minnie was starting in the fall, thumped the animal's pale stomach. "If we cut it open, I bet it's got somebody's arm or leg inside."

Minnie's eyes swelled like Coke-bottle caps. "You think?"

"It's my best guess."

"Charlie . . ." Minnie said hesitantly, "do you know all about sea creatures because your dad's a navy captain?"

He rubbed at one of his strong arms. "Naw, he

hasn't told me anything. I just read enough about sharks to know they hate people."

Mr. Panzer, who was rumored to be crazy, laughed. "They don't hate people."

"Some do . . . sir," the teenager said.

Minnie smiled and blinked. "Bet you might be right about it having a leg inside."

Carter said, "Minnie, he doesn't know what he's talking about."

"So, what do you think it's eaten, smarty-pants?"

"Probably fish."

"Right," Charlie scoffed. "Where do you get your information from?"

"From comic books," Minnie told the boy.

Mr. Panzer bent down and touched the shark's gooey nose. "Unless you want to look some more, why don't you kids go argue somewhere else?"

Charlie Dane said, "Sorry. We want to look, sir."

Carter circled the shark again. He leaned onto his toes and hovered over the head. The slit-eyes and hole-puncher teeth gave him the chills. He settled on his heels and squatted to touch the animal's bloated stomach. It was so hard that he wondered if Charlie might be right. Maybe the shark had eaten an arm and a leg and even a whole person. It seemed fat.

Sylvia walked up behind Carter and whispered, "You're right. I bet it's filled with fish."

Carter smiled at his sister's friend, whose dark, sympathetic face caused his heart to pound out of control. Sylvia had high cheekbones and a natural tan on account of her father being part Indian, from a tribe that had gotten shoved out of Norfolk a long time before. Looking at her excited him so much that a surprise burp clattered up from his guts and into his throat, forcing him to swallow it back. "Thanks, Sylvia," he rasped.

Shortly, the three of them started back home, walking barefoot through the bubbly rinse of waves. It was almost dark, and in the remaining light, fat raindrops began falling. Similar to tiny meteors, they slapped when they hit the water and sand. Carter said, "You think aliens are dropping these on us?"

"Dropping what?" Minnie asked.

"These," he explained, indicating the rain.

"The raindrops?"

"Yeah."

"Of course not."

"But they're big-sized."

"You think aliens are the only reason they could be like that?"

Sylvia said, "There aren't any aliens in space, except for maybe on Mars."

Carter told her, "Actually, we don't know for sure aliens aren't hiding behind the moon."

"I . . . I suppose —" Sylvia said, but she was interrupted by a violent streak of lightning that scorched the dark clouds above the bay, jagging down and striking a huge red channel buoy. A split second later, thunder trembled the beach.

"It's an invasion!" Carter screamed, and started running.

At first, the terrified girls were behind him, then they passed by, their feet kicking sand into his face as they tore up and through the dunes, around the house, and to the high front porch where Mr. and Mrs. Johnston rested on their hammock, watching the flat, heavy clouds overtake the southeastern end of Willoughby Spit and the amusement park. Down the block, near Sylvia's house, the lights along Ocean View Avenue glowed as if it were midnight, while flagpole wires tapped steadily in the wind and the Johnstons' back screen door creaked open and shut. More lightning flashed, and the world seemed to be getting x-rayed.

Carter spat sand from his mouth. "It's an alien invasion," he told his parents.

"Thought so," Mr. Johnston replied, sipping his beer.

"You did, Ray?" Mrs. Johnston asked, a smile barely adjusting her face.

"Yeah. I could tell."

"What're we going to do?" Carter wondered.

Mr. Johnston lifted a hand. "Surrender, I suppose."

Carter studied both parents. "But . . . it's just a storm, isn't it?"

His father sat up slowly, his narrow elbows slipping through the weave of the hammock. "You mean to tell me it's not an alien invasion?"

Carter smiled. "Dad, stop."

Mr. Johnston put his beer to his withered lips and

swallowed a few gulps. "Carter," he said, chuckling, "you're wonderful."

Minnie, who was leaning against one of the porch roof's columns, said, "Dad, why would you tell him that when you know he's just stupid?"

Chapter
SEVEN

Sylvia sat at Carter and Minnie's kitchen table, her shoeless feet swinging wildly and brushing across the grit on the linoleum tiles. She couldn't stop talking. The Korean War was officially over, and her father was probably coming home soon. "When he gets back, I bet we go to the park every night for two weeks. He loves the roller coaster and especially cotton candy. He likes the Ferris wheel and bumper cars and most of all —"

Mr. Johnston, who was leaning against a counter, mumbled, "Be nice to have him around."

Carter said, "I don't get how the war can just stop."

His mother, who was as excited as Sylvia, said, "They signed an armistice agreement."

"I don't know what that is."

"It's a truce," Minnie told Carter. "It says they won't fight anymore."

Mr. Johnston, who'd been laboring to breathe since he'd woken, lowered himself into a chair alongside the kitchen counter. He looked down at his knees, which resembled the lumpy joints on a large bird. "The war's been in stalemate for two years. All we were doing was killing young people, boys who wouldn't die otherwise. It's time to call an end to it."

"But we didn't win," Carter argued, surprised by his father, who'd been injured fighting Nazis in Italy and, later, had fought all the way to Germany with the U.S. First Army.

"Doesn't matter. This isn't about Hitler or Pearl Harbor. The North Koreans aren't going to bomb the coast or spread fascism across Europe." He lowered his scraggly head down into one of his hands. "This country's been fighting too long. I gave four healthy years to liberating Europe so that kids your age wouldn't have to worry about dying, least not in a war."

Carter nodded, but he didn't think it was right to quit on something so easily. It seemed like that was all his father did anymore, quit and laugh about it.

Sylvia giggled. "I'm . . . I'm just glad my dad might be coming home. You know, sometimes I can barely remember how he looks except for pictures."

Minnie told her, "He looks a little Mexican."

"Sort of, yeah."

Mrs. Johnston turned toward her husband; her eyes narrowed. "Ray? You okay?"

Carter and Minnie's dad shook his head, causing the butterscotch candy cane he substituted for a cigarette to fall from his mouth and onto the front of his shirt. "No," he gasped. He leaned forward and fell to the floor, landing on his knees. "I'm dizzy, and I can't breathe so hot. Was hurting this morning and . . ." Unable to finish his thought, he stretched back and put an arm on the chair seat.

Gloria Johnston rushed over and helped her husband rise. "Let's get you to bed," she said.

His head lolled on his neck. "How about out front? I could sit in the chaise lounge. I'd rather be there."

Mrs. Johnston nearly dragged him through the house, kids following.

"Might throw up," he told his wife.

She glanced back at her daughter. "Minnie, get a pail from under the kitchen sink."

The wide front porch looked out on their neighbors' homes, bungalows that were also on stilts. At the bottom of the wooden porch steps was their front yard, which was a scraggly patch of Bermuda grass that ended at their concrete street, which didn't look like a street at all, since it was nearly completely hidden under a thin coat of sand. Carter helped his mother get his father into the lounge chair.

"Dad," Carter said, "your candy's stuck to your shirt."

Mr. Johnston smiled. "Tear it off and put it in my mouth. Maybe it'll stop me from puking."

"Ray?" Mrs. Johnston spoke fearfully, cupping her

husband's saggy-skinned cheek. "You want me to call somebody?"

He nodded his head. "I think you should."

Minnie came out the screen door with a bowl. "Is this too small?"

Mrs. Johnston said, "It's okay." She took a deep breath and adjusted her skirt. "Why . . . why don't you kids go down to the beach and explore or swim or something?"

Minnie said, "Do we have to?"

"Yes."

Minnie and Sylvia reluctantly started down the steps, but Carter lingered for a moment. "Dad, does it really hurt so much?"

"Hurts like hell. Hurts worse than when my butt got torn up in Italy." Mr. Johnston ran a hand across his runny nostrils, and Carter wondered if he was crying. "Go on and play on the beach. This'll pass."

His boy hesitated.

"Carter," his mom said, "you need to go."

He nodded and lurched through the screen door, up the steps, and to his room, where he found his bathing suit.

Out on the shore, Sylvia and Minnie sat at the glassy water's edge. Carter came down from the house, digging his shins through the line of clutter, shells, sea grass, and driftwood that formed during storms and high tide. It was getting hot again, and a steamy curtain of air hung across the Chesapeake Bay so that a navy ship heading for sea appeared almost perfectly camouflaged. Straight overhead, the sun seemed to glint and burn behind frosted glass.

Minnie said, "Are you worried, Carter?"

He splashed into the calm water. "No."

"You sure?"

"Yeah."

"He'll be fine."

"Except for how he's quitting."

"He's not quitting."

"He always says, 'I'm not dying, yet.' 'I'm trying to enjoy my time.' 'I'll miss you guys.' Junk like that. He's quitting like crazy, Minnie. It's so stupid."

She rubbed a handful of water down one of her legs. "He's lived like a year and a half more than he was supposed to. He wants to stay alive, but he can't. Doctors say it's impossible."

"Nothing's impossible."

"Some things are."

Carter turned and waded into the polished-looking Chesapeake Bay. Except for the disturbance his body made, there was barely a ripple on the water. No wind blew. Carter closed his eyes, then opened them wide as they would go. A few feet away, he saw a stinging nettle and dove around it and started splashing through the water angrily.

He was fifty yards away before Minnie and Sylvia got up and followed him. Furious, he kept going for nearly a mile before he quit, dragging himself from the water and sitting silently on the beach. His narrow, tanned body was covered in red splotches from stinging nettles so that he looked to have five to ten big pink birthmarks.

Minnie said, "Carter, you're scaring me."

"I'm fine," he promised, jealous that Sylvia was getting her father back just as theirs seemed to be leaving.

Chapter EIGHT

Ray Johnston spent three nights in Willoughby Motors before his condition got so bad that an ambulance carried him to the Marine hospital for veterans, which was different from the army hospital across the water in Hampton. It was located in downtown Norfolk, and once he got there, his health seemed to deteriorate, causing him to slip in and out of sleep. When he was awake, he stared blankly through the window near his bed, which looked out over four dry-docked ships, unbelievably huge vessels that had been lifted out of the water on giant platforms similar to the bun under a hot dog.

Spread out on both sides of Ray Johnston were rows of veterans from World Wars I and II and the Korean War. They were so sick that only a few would survive.

The long wards smelled, which made Carter feel sad for his father. Also, the place was scattered full of disagreeable employees who smoked and pushed carts as if they were wheelbarrows full of cow manure. Carter figured his dad's condition was worse just because of the place. But his father couldn't have stayed at Willoughby Motors any longer. He'd needed oxygen and monitoring, and the car dealership couldn't fill its showroom with medical equipment.

"Gloria," Mr. Johnston rasped, his narrow face framed by a dirty pillow. "Thanks for bringing the kids."

Tears rolled down her broad cheeks. "They wanted to see you."

He lifted a hand. "Hey, now, don't cry. I'll be up and around soon. Already, I made plans for when I walk out of here."

Carter and Minnie's mom dabbed and scrunched her runny nose with a tissue. "Did you?"

"I got big plans. Fun . . . fun things I want to do. Okay, sweetheart?"

"Okay."

"Okay, Minnie?"

"I know, Dad."

"You hear me, Carter?"

Carter's eyes remained locked on the wheels of his father's bed.

"Carter? Did you hear me?"

"Yes, sir."

"Look at me."

He obeyed.

"I'll be home in less than a week, and I got plans for us to have a good time."

"Yes, sir."

Mr. Johnston pointed a shaky finger right at him. "Quit moping. This is no tragedy. Don't fool yourself. Tragedies are unexpected. It was a tragedy when we first heard, but we've expected this. Fact is, we expect I'll die someday soon, but this time I'll be coming home."

"Yes, sir."

And somehow, Mr. Johnston was almost exactly right. Within the week, he clawed his way back from the edge of death. His lungs, which had been on the verge of stopping, regained their elasticity and strength, while his heart relocated its missing rhythm. One week later than he had predicted, he was released. Just to show off, he walked through the front doors of the hospital looking terrible but using nothing but a cane and ignoring the crotchety nurse who demanded he ride in a wheelchair.

Arthritic and emaciated, he huffed and puffed and climbed into the family's tiny Henry J automobile, wincing as he adjusted his bony rear on the hard springs. "Guess this car could be worse. It could have wooden seats, huh?"

Carter touched him on the shoulder. "Don't they feel like wood?"

"Yup."

Mrs. Johnston settled her skirt about her legs and started the car. "Ready, Ray?"

"Oh, yeah," he told her as he loosened a butterscotch candy cane from its wrapper.

They drove down past tall office buildings and turned on Granby Street, which they took all the way to Ocean View Avenue. "Minnie's got a boyfriend," Carter blurted as they passed the amusement park.

His father turned. "A boyfriend?"

"It's Charlie Dane from down the beach. He's going to be in her high school. The other night, he came over and sat with her on the porch, and today his mother took them to the movies. That's why she's not here."

"Well, all right. Good for her."

Mrs. Johnston said, "I won't let her go to his house yet. I only met his mother today."

Mr. Johnston said, "Trust Minnie. She's a good girl."

Carter told him, "I wouldn't be so sure."

"Figured you'd feel that way."

"Did you know Charlie thinks he's an expert on sharks?"

"That dirty bastard." Mr. Johnston cackled hoarsely.

Mrs. Johnston slapped one of his arms. "Ray, no gutter talk."

"But, Gloria, I got a whole list of words and sayings

from the boys around me at the hospital. They were great cussers, except for a guy who'd been a military priest."

"Ray, if you start teaching Minnie and Carter to talk that way, I'll carry you right back to the hospital. I'm not kidding."

He lifted his hands. "That's a fate worse than death. I'm telling you, I'll never cuss again."

At home, it took him five difficult minutes to get up the house's long front steps and five more to settle on the porch hammock. "Could use a beer, Gloria," he joked.

"I'll get you a glass of water," she said, and went inside.

Carter looked down the street, where cars passed on the way to the ferry. A streetcar clanked and clattered by. He turned and sat on an aluminum chair beside his father. "I've been swimming a lot. I can go a mile."

"A mile? Now, that's impressive."

Carter smiled. "Bet most normal people can't go for so long." He rubbed his hands and scooted forward in his chair. "Mom was late from work yesterday. I noticed but Minnie didn't. You . . . you think she might've gone somewhere else? You know?"

"I don't."

"You think she went to see her family?"

He blinked his eyes as if his vision was blurry. "Oh, you mean could she have swum out to visit her family?"

"Yeah."

"Maybe."

Carter hesitated. "You think she really might be from Atlantis?"

"I can't say for sure she's not."

"Granddad Wheatley had smooth skin. Like a fish."

"It was smooth, and he acted funny sometimes, too. But fish have scales."

"Oh, yeah."

Carter's mother came out the door. "What are you two talking about?" she asked, glancing from her husband to her son.

"Atlantis," Mr. Johnston answered, his head wobbling weakly, so that he rested it back. He removed his butterscotch like it was a cigarette, then he took the glass from her hand and drank back some cold water, which ran all over his chin.

She looked confused. "Atlantis. The underwater city?"

"Tha'ssss right," he slurred, handing her the glass. "You . . . you know it, dear?"

"I've read some things."

Carter told her, "That's where the Sub-Mariner's from."

"I've looked through those comic books," she informed him.

"You have?"

"They're always on your bed."

Carter's close-together, sneaky eyes narrowed, and he said, "Okay, Mom," stretching out the words, sure that he knew her secret. He looked slyly at his father, but Mr. Johnston was sound asleep.

Chapter
NINE

A few nights later, after dinner, Carter, Minnie, and Sylvia wandered down the long, pale strip of beach, silvery oyster shells gleaming in the rising moonlight. Up on the boardwalk, they met up with Pruitt, who'd waited for them alongside a bench that faced the water. The four of them wandered through the amusement park, the scent of peanuts and cotton candy drifting on the air. They stopped and watched sailors arm-wrestle at a booth. Pushing on, they saw people getting their palms read, and when they heard a commotion in the bumper-car corral, they rushed over to see what had happened.

"Hold on! Hold on!" a large amusement park employee with one arm shouted as he carried a rusty first-aid kit across the floor. A girl had gotten her hand slightly injured between cars, and he delicately applied a Band-Aid to one of her skinned knuckles.

Pruitt looked at his three friends and said, "You guys don't have any money at all?"

They shook their heads.

"Wish you did."

"Yeah," they agreed.

Pruitt said, "You wanna do like last time and go watch people getting off the roller coaster?" His eyes lingered on Sylvia.

Minnie asked, "Why would we want to see that again?"

"'Cause it's kind of funny when people look sick."

"What's funny about it?"

Carter said, "Can you tell she's annoyed my mom wouldn't let her see her new boyfriend today?"

Minnie replied, "Carter, do you always have to be such a goof?"

"You must be in love or something. You're always doing stuff with Charlie now."

She leaned against a wall. "For your information, I've only done a total of four things with him."

"Seems like more."

"That's because you can't count."

"I can count, Minnie. It's because you always talk about him is why."

"Least it's better than talking about comic-book characters."

Carter glanced from Sylvia to Pruitt and back. "I like other things, too. I . . . I looked at the newspaper yesterday."

"He read the funnies," Minnie told them.

Embarrassed, Carter took a step backward. "Come on, Pruitt, let's go watch people get off the roller coaster." He paused to give Sylvia a nervous smile. "You . . . you want to come with us?"

"That's all right."

"You can."

Minnie laughed cruelly. "For your information, she likes you less than I do."

Minnie's comment struck Carter like one of her

powerful punches. His mood momentarily injured, he weaved through the crowds alongside Pruitt, till they came to the white picket fence surrounding the base of the roller-coaster tracks, where bright lights sparkled similar to the marquee on Norfolk's opera house. Behind the fence, a roller-coaster cart screeched past, its steel wheels squealing loudly as it jolted sharply and started up a long incline. Carter and Pruitt kept to the edge of the fence till they got to a popular picnic area just below the boarding ramp to the ride, where a crowd of teenagers always camped out to spy nauseated passengers.

Carter found an empty lamppost and scrambled up onto the fancy base like he was a pirate on the mast of a sailing ship. They watched passengers on a roller-coaster cart disembark, but everyone seemed fine. Holding tight to the pole, Carter glanced into the starry sky, where a seagull swept diagonally across the full moon. Watching for another, he said to Pruitt, "Wouldn't it be cool if we could fly, and I went over and grabbed a roller-coaster cart that was full of people?"

Pruitt wiped at his sweaty brow with the tail of his shirt. "Why would you want to?"

"Because."

"But where would you take it?"

"I don't know." He thought and realized that if he managed something like that, it would be even better than swimming across Hampton Roads. "I'd fly over to show my dad."

Pruitt thought about where he'd go. "I'd . . . I'd probably show Sylvia."

Carter exclaimed, "Sylvia?"

"Yeah."

"Why her?"

"'Cause, I . . . I think she's a little all-right looking. Hey, can I get up there?"

Ignoring his friend's request, Carter said, "Pruitt, she's older than you and part Indian to boot!"

"So?"

"Also, she's my sister's best friend."

"You're just mad about what Minnie said."

"Am not. It's just that Sylvia's never going to like you, so you ought to get a crush on another girl."

Somebody behind them grunted, "Carter!"

Carter adjusted himself on the pole.

Charlie Dane said, "Is your sister around?"

"She went home already," he lied.

Charlie slipped his hands into his pockets and lolled his head to one side.

"What's the matter, Charlie? Did you want to try and put the moves on her tonight?"

"What're you talking about?"

"You know? You play football, and your dad's a captain in the navy, so you probably think you can make out with any girl you want."

"No, I don't."

Carter twisted and watched passengers climb from a roller-coaster cart.

"Hey, I don't," Charlie promised.

Carter got down from the base of the light pole to let Pruitt take a turn. Standing on the boardwalk, he scooted up close to Charlie and real softly, like a gangster, hissed, "All I can say is that you better not do anything like that, because my dad's a boxer, and he's taught me things. Plus, he might get mad and want to beat you up himself. If you're mean to Minnie, it'd be a big mistake."

"I don't plan on being mean."

Carter dropped his head to study his shoes. He scuffed at the boardwalk with the worn rubber soles. His shorts shifted in a cool breeze that caused helium balloons and tall hairstyles to sway. "You . . . you just make sure you don't. Me and Dad can box like crazy. Like six months ago, he knocked out Rocky Marciano in an exhibition match. He could knock you out in a second."

Charlie seemed confused. "But . . . Minnie said your dad's dying."

Carter shook his head. "She makes things up. She has to watch out for him every second. He'd go crazy if you were mean to her."

"Well, I don't plan on being mean. I like her."

From his place on the light pole, Pruitt said, "Hey, I think a kid's about to barf."

Chapter
TEN

Mr. Johnston lifted a hand and leaned dramatically on his cane, as if his legs barely functioned. His shirt billowed about his starved body. "Don't buy the place out!" he instructed.

"I won't!" Carter told him. Alone, he walked next to the bright green water, kicking through the small waves that rushed up the shore. Without looking, he passed the amusement park and continued on down the boiling-hot beach till Harrison's Pier loomed in front of him like a scratchy line drawn on paper.

Getting closer, he ran his eyes over and over the catwalk part of the pier, which stretched far out into the bay and bristled with fishermen and their tall rods.

Near the heavy wooden pilings, Carter scurried up toward the dunes, crossing over a small bump before stepping onto a wooden pathway that led to the bridge connecting the pier to the shore. Ahead, suspended over the water, were the restaurant and store as well as the ticket counter, where people paid for their right to fish. Behind those things was the long, long fishing section.

Passing up the bridge, Carter stared at the beach, then the water, through the cracks between the planks, so that because he wasn't paying attention he stubbed his toe on a warped slat. Outside the restaurant, he rubbed fiercely at the pain to make it go away. As he worked, he saw his neighbor Mr. Owens, with Papa Bear at his feet, seated in the restaurant and encircled by half-naked fishermen who were chewing through hamburgers and guzzling Cokes. The old, well-dressed man sipped a cup of coffee and read *Tarzan, Lord of the Apes*, while the Chihuahua snoozed beside the pointed tips of his polished shoes.

Carter crossed the walkway and passed through the door of Harrison's Fishing Store. Rounded refrigerators hummed loudly, mostly stocked full of bloodworms. Near those were large tubs gurgling with bait, different-size minnows and squid. Right down the center of the store, on long racks, were fishing rods, while lures and reels and fillet knives were displayed inside chipped-glass cases. On the wall above those were lineups of hooks and sinkers and a cardboard poster covered with black combs and decorated with a drawing of a muscly man bending one in half. On shelves and beneath windows were stacks of buckets for fish and bait. And, as usual, the place smelled like dirt and plants, which Carter never understood.

He scuffed directly to the wire magazine racks and twirled them till he located the comic books. He found the least-wrinkled copy of *Young Men*, which contained stories about the Sub-Mariner, Captain America, and the Human Torch. He took a minute to study its thrilling cover before carrying it and some war comics to the cash register.

The guy who rang him up said, "First of those we sold all week. Nobody's buying superheroes anymore."

"Not even *Young Men*?"

"Not even *Batman*."

Glancing back at the rack, Carter said, "That's bad, huh?"

The guy handed him his change. "We'll live."

Carter left the store feeling light with excitement over having three new stories to read. Smiling widely, he went into the restaurant and purchased himself a multicolored jawbreaker, which he stuck in his mouth as he headed for the door.

"Carter?" Mr. Owens said, looking up from his novel.

With his tongue, Carter pushed the jawbreaker into a cheek so that he looked like a squirrel. "Mr. Owens?"

"How's your father?"

"Good."

"Out of the hospital, I noticed."

"Yes, sir. We picked him up last Saturday."

Mr. Owens set his book down on the tabletop. "He's got nine lives, your dad."

"Nine lives of what, sir?"

Mr. Owens lifted a wrinkled hand and smoothed down his mustache. "It means he's tough. He's tough like a cat. People say it takes nine tries to finally get rid of those fur-ball nuisances."

Carter reached into his mouth and removed the slobbery jawbreaker with a thumb and finger. He lowered it to his side, opposite the hand that held the bag of comics. "You think he's tough?"

"I do. He's been very sick for a long time."

"Not so sick."

"He's pretty sick. That's the fact of the matter."

Carter peered at his wet candy, which looked a lot like a tiny model of planet Earth. "I think he exaggerates a little."

"I don't."

"If he really wanted, don't you think he could get better?"

Mr. Owens leaned back and watched Papa Bear's sleeping form rise and fall with each breath. The old man thought on his coffee cup, which he picked up. "Actually, I don't know. I'm no doctor."

"I don't know, either," Carter said. He couldn't think of what else he should say, so he lifted the brown bag. "I got new comic books. We're going to read them this afternoon."

Mr. Owens nodded. "Did you get that one about the prince fella?"

"Yes, sir." Carter raised the jawbreaker to his mouth but didn't stuff it in. He was watching Papa Bear inhale and exhale. "Mr. Owens, I can hold my breath for two and a half minutes. You think that's a lot?"

"Seems like a long time."

"Does it almost seem impossible?"

"Almost, yes."

Carter popped in the jawbreaker. "Thanks, Mr. Owens."

"Okay, Carter. Tell your mother and father I said hello."

"Yes, sir."

On the beach, Carter ran for a time. He went along near the dunes and every so often dashed up and down a few. Then, filled with energy and happiness, he jammed the shrinking jawbreaker into a cheek and sprinted down and jumped an old log near the water, landing with a splat so that three sandpipers flew into the air. He stopped and watched the birds fly along the beach. He thought about how Prince Namor shot around using the little wings on his ankles. Curious, Carter sat down and lifted his legs to check around for tiny feathers. He looked hard, but his ankles were pretty regular except that one had a bump, like acne, on it, which made him wonder, after a time, if a wing was just starting to sprout.

He got up and jumped at the sky. He landed. He pointed his arms, ran, and jumped again. He tried a few different takeoff styles but never left the ground for longer than a second.

Figuring the wing still had to grow, he walked on, approaching the park and its pavilions and comfortable boardwalk. He went up and shuffled through the small crowds before he realized that most people were looking north along Willoughby Spit. He followed their gaze and saw that an aircraft carrier, destroyers, and a few battleships had rounded the point and were cruising out to sea. He turned and looked toward the naval base, way beyond Willoughby Bay. Above where the docks were located, he could see clouds of exhaust pumping high into the air.

He wanted to ask someone what was happening. He wanted to know if the communists had a flotilla of warships and submarines offshore ready to blast Norfolk's naval base with a nuclear bomb or a barrage of shells. If there were enemies coming, nobody on Willoughby Spit would have a good place to hide. Nobody's house had a basement. Worse, though, was how sick his father was. His dad would never survive an attack.

Carter rushed along the boardwalk, his legs a blur, his feet thunking lightly across the planks. Where it ended, he jumped down the steps and onto the beach and ran as fast as he could. Spread across the dunes like scattered shrubs were various residents who had left their homes and stood looking out at the ships. Carter hurried on, till he saw his sister and dad standing atop a grassy mound behind their home.

Staggering up, Carter asked, "Is there a war?"

"Doubt it," his father croaked. "Haven't heard any-thing."

Minnie, who looked pale, told him, "It's . . . it's probably okay. Don't worry."

Carter studied her nice face, and for the first time realized that whenever he was scared she tried to make him feel better. He suddenly appreciated that. Still, it wouldn't work because he could tell she was scared, too. He shifted his intense gaze to his father. "Shouldn't we find out what's happening?"

Mr. Johnston dug at the sand with his cane, then gazed toward the peninsula where the U.S. Navy's Atlantic Fleet was docked. Long pillars of black engine exhaust rose high into the sky, mingling with the blue. Swaying back around, he smiled and said, "I don't hear air-raid sirens. I think we're going to be fine."

"What about communists?" Carter asked, wor-ried. "They're everywhere."

Mr. Johnston licked his chapped lips. "They aren't everywhere. There isn't one in our house, and I'd bet there's not one on all of Willoughby Spit. It's that buffoon, Senator McCarthy. He thinks we're overrun with communists and is getting people stirred up about nothing. I'm sure he'd be happy to know he's terrifying kids now, the idiot."

Their father took a long, raspy whiff of salty air. Forcing a smile, he said, "There aren't any enemies out there. The ships aren't moving fast enough. Bet . . . bet there's a storm coming."

"You think?"

"Before big storms, they always send the fleet out to sea."

Carter studied the gray war vessels.

His dad said, "Did you get the comic books? That's what I want to know."

"I got them."

"Well, all right." He grinned even wider. "Minnie, you interested in reading one?"

"No, thanks."

With a trembling hand, he brushed wisps of dark hair off her shoulders. "You okay?"

Without looking at him, she said, "I'm sort of scared."

Carter shot a fearful look at his father.

Mr. Johnston propped his cane against a leg, and,

as if he was christening his children, he touched a shuddering, bony hand to both of their heads. "It's okay. I promise."

Carter felt his father's weak fingers shiver against his hair, and he wondered if his dad was so calm because he was dying no matter what.

Chapter
ELEVEN

Around midnight, the planes that guarded Norfolk from an enemy attack began barreling down the runways and taking flight. Masses of them circled the city and its neighborhoods prior to falling into formation and roaring over Ocean View Avenue, skimming the rooftops and rattling windowpanes as they hurtled away. Terrified that their departure confirmed his worst fears, Carter crept down the hall and into Minnie's stagnant room. He shook her.

"What?" she whispered, her sweaty hair pressed like a small animal against one of her ears.

"The planes are leaving from the naval base."

She sat up.

"You . . . you think we're about to get attacked?" he asked.

"I . . . I don't think," she told him.

"We need to tell Mom and Dad," he said.

She got up, and together they went down the hallway to their parents' room. Without knocking, they pushed the door wide and jabbed one of their father's scrawny arms. He didn't stir. They tried again, gave up, and went around to their mother.

She opened her eyes. "Minnie? Carter?"

He said, "The planes at the naval base are flying somewhere. I think communists are attacking."

"No, sweetheart. No, they aren't," she whispered back. "A storm is coming. The navy's moving them up the coast. I promise."

Minnie stood quietly before asking, "How do you know?"

"Before bed, your father and I heard it on the

radio. There's a hurricane down near the Carolinas that's the cause. I promise."

"But why're they moving the planes?"

"Because that's what they do. It's so they aren't stuck on the runway during a storm if they're needed."

Minnie appeared satisfied, but Carter said, "You think they're just saying that?"

"I don't." His mother gently touched his chin for a second. "There's no reason to worry. Go back to bed, okay?"

Minnie took Carter's hand and led him to her room, where she shut her door partway and asked, "You feel better now?"

He didn't know. For years he'd listened to the planes whine up and down, believing that if they took flight, he'd probably die. He'd thought that way for so long that it was hard to imagine it wasn't true. "Maybe Mom's heard there's a war, and she's acting that way because she can't do anything about it."

"She'd try and get us on a ferry."

"Not if Dad can't be moved. She'd maybe let us all get killed together."

"She wouldn't."

More planes flew over, and Carter and Minnie listened as their props pulled them slower than the jets, out toward the Atlantic Ocean. He felt slightly faint. "I think we're about to get bombed."

"No, we're not."

Dizzy, he considered jumping beneath his sister's bed, except that their house was on stilts, and in a big explosion it would probably just tumble over and smash into pieces. "Your hair looks funny," was all he managed to say.

Minnie pulled the knot from around her ear and pushed it over a shoulder. "Mom doesn't lie. I never heard her lie, not once."

"But she won't tell us what Dad's dying of. Maybe she's doing the same sort of thing about there being a war. Maybe she's not telling us."

Minnie, who'd regained her composure, didn't hesitate. "She's not telling us because there isn't one."

In the dim light, Carter dropped his head, turned, and peered at his sister through a partially cracked mirror. "You . . . you want to come sit in my room for a while?"

She nodded, and they went down the hallway, where Carter scrambled onto his bed and Minnie crossed her legs and sat on the floor. Together, they waited for bombs to fall, and before two hours passed, both had fallen asleep, Minnie on Carter's thin, oval carpet. While they slept, before the morning light, a hard wind stirred and got the curtains around Carter's windows to snap and ripple like flags on the hood of a fast-moving car. The noise didn't wake either of them, though.

Around eight, Mr. Johnston leaned in the doorway and tapped his cane against his son's floor. He rasped, "Time to rise and shine. Haul yourselves out of sleep. It's late."

Carter lifted his head.

"Before your mom goes to work, we're taking her for breakfast at the Southern Pancake House."

Swallowing, Carter adjusted onto his side. "Why?"

"Because it'll be nice."

While his father watched, Carter struggled from knotted sheets and looked through his dresser for a shirt to go with the shorts he'd worn to sleep. He found one, and as he slid it over his head, it dawned on him that they'd survived the night. Behind him, his curtains popped and fluttered wildly, and he twisted and stared between the jumping flaps of fabric. The Chesapeake Bay was cluttered with whitecaps and wind-driven waves. Also, it had risen to cover half the beach, which always happened in bad weather. He felt like a chowderhead for being so terrified the night before.

"Why'd your sister sleep in here?" Mr. Johnston asked, tilting against the wall for support.

Carter adjusted his gaze onto Minnie's snoring form. Sometimes, he liked her in a way that, if someone asked him to, he couldn't ever explain.

"She was a little scared," he said.

By nine, all four members of the Johnston family were settled atop the hard seats of the Henry J automobile. Mrs. Johnston strapped on a wrinkly rain bonnet and directed the car down the sandy blocks. Alongside Sylvia's grandmother's house, she turned onto Ocean View Avenue and gunned it. They gained speed, and their neighbors' homes became a colorful, complicated blur. Block after block, the rocket ornament on the hood of the car whistled loudly in the sideways-gusting wind. For a few minutes, Carter closed his eyes and imagined that they were heading for orbit inside a Flash Gordon spaceship.

Mrs. Johnston pulled into one of the new shopping plazas at Ward's Corner. Cautiously, she pointed the hood at the Southern Pancake House's heavy, dark, wooden doors and stopped in a space in front of them, a few businesses down from Hoffheimer Shoes, where she worked. Setting the brake, she fetched her handbag from under her seat, paused, and peered across at her husband, who was working hard to exit and looked about as bad as he ever had. "Ray, maybe after breakfast I should drive you guys back home."

He stopped. His hair looked like a rooster's comb. "I wouldn't hear of such a thing. I . . . I got big plans for today. I'll be fine."

She didn't seem as certain as he did. "Don't overextend yourself. That's all I ask."

"I won't," he promised, wrestling to pull his cane out after him.

In the dimly lit restaurant, Mr. Johnston stared at the glob of whipped butter melting on his pancakes, then he took a few difficult bites. Every so often, he lifted his coffee cup to his shriveled lips and sipped and winced like he was swallowing splinters. After that, he usually grimaced and adjusted atop his chair. Finally, he closed his eyes and summoned strength and will from places inside of himself that had seemed vanished. "Feel . . . feel like I rode here on a horse," he declared, forcing power and humor into his voice. "T-tell me, could that car of ours be much worse? It rides like a tank that I got a lift on during the war." He pointed his fork shakily at his daughter. "Okay, here and now, kids, I'm directing your mom to dump the Henry J for a better car as soon as she gets the check from my life insurance policy. I want you to make sure she does that, you understand?"

"Dad, stop," said Minnie.

Carter said, "Yeah."

"All I'm saying is" — he looked at his wife — "Gloria, you don't deserve to drive around on such hard seats. This morning they nearly took my life, but, for God's sake, the Henry J has hurt my ass from day one." He smiled.

Mrs. Johnston grinned back. "Ray, your language has gotten terrible."

"Yes, it has," he said proudly, and jammed a hunk of pancake, which he obviously had no desire to eat, into his mouth. Turning, he spit it into a napkin. "But . . . I won't allow you to take me back to a hospital, least not a veterans' hospital. I'd rather die in a goddamned garbage can."

Carter, who was seated alongside his dad, liked when his father cussed. He figured that people who cussed didn't think they were going to die, since they wouldn't be allowed in heaven as a result of their bad language. It made Carter feel so good that he guzzled his second enormous cup of hot chocolate with whipped cream on top. Plopping the cup down on its saucer, he stabbed at the remaining slabs of pancake on his plate.

At the front of the restaurant, the wind opened and closed the door, causing their napkins to flutter occasionally, as though the family was eating in front of an oscillating fan. Carter listened to the gusts and wondered if the hurricane would hit Norfolk.

After breakfast, Minnie and Carter walked their

mother down to the shoe store, where Gloria Johnston stood in the doorway, alongside the machine
that x-rayed people's feet. She leaned and kissed each
child on the cheek. "You guys watch your father and
make sure he doesn't begin to wear out."

Minnie said, "We won't be able to tell."

Mrs. Johnston didn't know what to say.

After climbing into the car, Mr. Johnston put the
key in the ignition but didn't start the engine. Alongside him, Minnie sat calmly while Carter, who was
located beside the passenger door, was busy explor-
ing everything within reach, like he'd never seen any
of it before.

"Stop, Carter!" Minnie finally demanded.

"Doing what?"

"Opening everything and moving around so
much."

"I'm not."

"Who is, then?"

Mr. Johnston made a show of nudging his daughter with an elbow. "Your brother's what they call
insane. We're going to drop him off at the mental

hospital downtown. The doctors'll treat him like a giant house pet. He'll eat from a dog dish and drink from a bowl. They'll put him in a padded room, where he'll have a hole in the ground for a toilet. And, worst of all, they won't allow him to wear anything but his underwear, so that he can't fashion a weapon and hurt the hospital staff."

Minnie grinned at her father. "I wish it was true."

"Dad," Carter said, "do they allow for giant bras in those places? I just want to know in case they want Minnie instead of me."

She slammed a fist into his arm.

Laughing, Mr. Johnston started the engine. He drove away as if he was in a hurry, gunning the Henry J through the streets of Norfolk. Right off, he headed downtown, past the opera house and Maury High School and into the Ghent section, with its mix of well-kept old buildings and places that seemed like King Kong had walked through kicking things over. On Princess Anne Boulevard, which led out of the city, they drove along, slowing when they got to a familiar walled area. Turning, they rifled around a cemetery's tiny lanes, then stopped beneath a huge, swaying oak that loomed over Mr. Johnston's mother's and father's tombstones.

"I don't want to be here," Minnie told him. "This isn't fun."

"It's going to be nice," Mr. Johnston promised, struggling to get from his seat.

Outside, Carter stood silently looking about at the thrashing trees and shrubs and blinking when a splash of water caught him in the eye. There was nothing he hated more than graveyards. He mumbled, "I never like coming here, either."

Mr. Johnston took a sputtery inhale. "Yeah, I realize that. Kids shouldn't like cemeteries. But we're here because it's important. It's important that you know about your grandparents, because they weren't from anywhere special or unique at all. In fact, they were nobodies, except they saved money during the Depression to send me to college, and they had personalities that filled everyone around them with good humor and hope. I was their only kid, and let me tell you, they overflowed my life with company and jokes and a feeling that I was wanted everywhere I went."

"They can't anymore," Minnie informed him.

"But they still do," he said, reaching into his pocket for a butterscotch candy cane. "They always do." The wind tugged at Ray Johnston's thinning copper hair, and he put the yellow stick to his lips. "I want you guys to get something from this. I want you to know that coming here, to this spot, isn't sad at all. It shouldn't be, either. I come here and I feel connected to two people. I come here and I don't get sad. I get happy. We're here to celebrate their lives, not to feel sad. Forget the crying. The same thing goes for me. If you cry over me, what a waste, because I'll have been a happy man who had a millionaire's type of fun with you guys and your drop-dead gorgeous mom."

Mr. Johnston took a second to slow his lungs. "Besides," he said, touching a hand flat to his chest, "I'll always be with you in memories and in your blood. You got me and my parents and your mom and her parents inside of you both, and that's a celebration of the past and our family."

Mr. Johnston raised his hands to the gray, fast-moving sky and smiled. "We're here to celebrate that my folks existed. Wasn't I lucky? Aren't I a lucky son of a bitch?"

Carter smiled.

Lowering his wiry arms, Mr. Johnston looked down at his parents' gravestones. "I remember my mom and dad chasing each other around our apartment like kids, tickling and teasing and rolling on the floor. Did I ever tell you, up until I was a teenager, when my dad spoke to me, he always used the funniest voice, like he was a frog? And Mom, during grade school, she'd dress me and my friends up any which way we wanted, like pirates and Sinbad and famous generals. Once a month, my dad boxed, too. I never was allowed to watch, but he'd get his butt whupped so bad and come home laughing the whole way. You know why?"

Minnie said, "Why?"

With difficulty, Mr. Johnston sat on the wet ground, resting his bony back against his mother's cold tombstone. "'Cause he had his chance to live and was loving every minute of it and wanted to give that to me. When all's said and done, see, all you leave is your memory, and if it's no good, what's the use? I want mine to be magic, just like my parents' memories are for me. I don't want tears. When you think of me, I want you to laugh so hard you wet your pants."

"Dad?" Minnie said, smiling for the first time.

As if he was too happy to hold anything, Mr. Johnston tossed his cane, which struck the front of the Henry J. "Whew!" he hollered. "Hey . . . hey, Minnie, sweetheart, I got a request. If you ever have a boy, you name him after me. Okay?"

"Okay," she said, and tears welled up from her eyelids.

"And, Carter, you keep reaching for things. You concentrate on being a superhero or an FBI agent or whatever. That's the kind of high-minded daydreaming I always respected. You reach and reach and enjoy the reaching, because it's all there is. It's all the fun you're going to get, so enjoy it."

Mr. Johnston lowered his head till his scraggly chin touched his chest. Feebly, he scooted sideways, and, with a skin-and-bone hand, he squeezed the edge of his father's tombstone, closing his eyes as tears inched down his grinning cheeks. "Let's go annoy all of Norfolk. Let's go raise the roof like we've never done. Then, when you guys get hungry again, let's get some burgers at Dumar's Drive-In. After that, well, God knows what. I . . . I might just buy your mother a new car. I might. I wouldn't put it past the three of us. Would you?"

"No," Minnie said.

Carter didn't reply. He didn't feel so good about things. What he knew as the wind beat against the three of them, and trees and shrubs bent back fiercely, was that he'd be lost without his dad. His father couldn't croak, because he'd be so lost he'd never be able to reach for anything amazing or even good. Not ever.

Chapter
TWELVE

As he roared from the cemetery, Mr. Johnston's health appeared to leave him with the suddenness of a deflating raft. Within an hour, the meager blaze in his eyes had disappeared. A strange weakness in his arms began to make it hard for him to grip the Henry J's steering wheel. Then a searing, tight pain started across his chest, worrying Minnie and Carter, who got out of the car and phoned their mother at her job. She took a cab to the parking lot they were in and drove them home. Then, to everyone's horror, after Mr. Johnston had labored to get out of the car, he collapsed painfully against the front steps.

Carefully, they moved Mr. Johnston to his bedroom. Due to his fall, his lip was swollen and his forehead was split above his nose. His rangy, frail body was bruised all over, and, every few minutes, pain caused his face to tighten into something that resembled a piece of coral.

That night, while the storm roamed the waters of the mid-Atlantic, Carter read comic books and scratched hard at his ankles. Later, as he drifted to fitful sleep, he thought about his mother's family and how her father breathed through a mask and had skin that appeared extra slick.

The following day, late in the afternoon, Carter watched as Sylvia and her grandmother drove off in the station wagon Minnie had helped them pack. In the early-morning hours, the slow-moving hurricane had wobbled and turned directly toward Virginia. It was forecast to plow diagonally into the coast by the evening. Shore communities along the ocean and the Chesapeake Bay were at risk from storm surge, high winds, and damaging surf. In fact, one of the very most exposed communities was Willoughby Spit, which clung delicately to the northwestern tip of Norfolk like a single fragile finger on an ancient statue. Some new residents and a few elderly folks, like Sylvia's grandmother, had decided to evacuate, but most people wanted to ride the storm out, as they'd ridden out others.

Carter's eyes stayed on the Chevrolet till it disappeared behind a series of homes, then he backed across the porch and opened the front door.

Since all the windows were shuttered tightly, the living room was dark. Holding his breath, he listened for his mom's footsteps on the floor above, but all he heard was the wooden shingles on the exterior walls of their home crackling and adjusting to the prying wind. He knew she was up there, though, because she refused to leave their father for more than a few minutes.

Looking over at his sister, who was reading, Carter asked, "Where're Sylvia and her grandmother going?"

Minnie adjusted on the faded, floral-patterned

couch. "Granby High School." She studied him for a moment. "Carter, you know how, at the amusement park, I said Sylvia likes you less than I do?"

He nodded.

"Well, she likes you more than that."

He could feel his cheeks warm.

"You like her, too, don't you?"

He said, "She's nice. For a girl."

Minnie pulled a pillow over her legs and sat silently for a few minutes before speaking very softly. "Yesterday, I got a feeling Dad recognized he was going to die today. You know? I heard that people know that sort of thing."

Her comment surprised him. "He's not dying. He feels bad, is all."

"I heard Mom talking on the phone."

Horrified, Carter spun around and pounded up the stairs, knocking on his parents' door. "Mom?" he said when she opened it.

"You want to talk to him?" she asked.

"What if I wait till tomorrow?"

"Maybe you better do it now."

He said, "Dad?"

Mr. Johnston replied, "Hey, Carter?" With an effort, he adjusted his battered face and smiled in his wild-eyed, enthusiastic way, like he might get up and light a firecracker under someone's chair.

Mrs. Johnston said, "I'm going to wait in the hallway."

After the door shut, Carter said, "Dad, I got to know, does Mom always go to work?"

Mr. Johnston gripped his son's narrow fingers. "I don't believe she does," he said, and tried to wink one of his swollen eyes but couldn't.

"Do you think Grampa Wheatley is from Atlantis, or partway from Atlantis?"

"Anything is possible."

"Dad," Carter whispered, "I'm . . . I'm going to show you something you won't believe. So don't die. Okay?"

"I'm trying not to."

"You won't believe it. I promise."

"Can't wait."

Carter backed out of the bedroom, stopping alongside his mother. "Are . . . are you from somewhere else?" he asked her.

"You know I am."

Carter said, "Dad's going to be better."

She mistook her son's promise for a question. "I don't know."

"He will," Carter said, hurrying to his room, where he changed into a bathing suit. In a flash, he went downstairs and called, "Bye, Minnie."

"Where're you going?"

"To see what's happening."

He banged out the door and ran across the porch and down the front steps. Circling around the house, he jogged sideways up on the dunes and alongside the battering water, which was breaking only a few feet away. He picked his way through the deafening gusts, something that took longer than he ever imagined. In time, he arrived at the point of Willoughby Spit, where, a few hundred yards away, the ferry launch was about to be overrun by tidal surge. Looking out past Fort Wool, he knew he was directly in line with the town of Hampton and Old Point Comfort with its famous Chamberlain Hotel, which was known for its large patio on the roof and verandas near the water for ballroom dancing. With dark, slate-colored clouds crowding the horizon and the sky, it was impossible to see, but he knew it was there.

In front of him, the waves were huge, dark green mountains with bottomless, wide valleys. The entire scene was tattered by the howling wind, which spread splashing water and bands of salty foam through the air like colorless streamers.

Blinking, Carter lifted off his T-shirt. In an instant, his long body broke out in goose bumps, which, as far as he could remember, never happened to the Sub-Mariner, even when he swam with icebergs. Still, he didn't get scared. He was about to do something great. He was going to show what a strong spirit could do and, in the process, become something that only his mother could guess.

Removing his sneakers, Carter fought the wind down a dune and stood in the tepid wash of waves. The white, churned water eddied around his ankles like they were tiny pilings. He went down farther, up to his knees, then to his waist. Watching the seam of his bathing suit turn dark, he didn't see the storm-driven swell that hit him square in the chest, knocking him backward. Underwater, he tried to turn and stand, but his feet skidded along the eroding sand, and, suddenly, he was out in the hurricane water and swimming.

As if he were a bottle, he rode the wild, heaving surface, sweeping high up to the top of monster-size waves and sinking low into their deep, deep troughs. He treaded water and snorted as salty foam blasted up his nostrils before ripping past. He searched desperately back toward the fading beach, where he thought he saw somebody yelling and waving. But then he was down in another trough and it didn't matter. He could hardly take a full breath and turned his head from the wind, in the direction of Fort Wool, which he saw in flashes, when he was at the top of a wave and hadn't yet been blinded by a fury of gusting spray.

He started swimming but quickly swallowed so much dark water that his throat hurt. He coughed and tried to get air, and a wave smashed down and drove him under into the thick, murky water, where the tides and currents tugged and pulled but weren't nearly as frightening as on the surface. He moved his arms and told himself to relax and breathe in like an Atlantian, but something inside wouldn't let him do it. Panicked, he swam desperately to the surface and broke into the humming air halfway up a wave. He coughed and took a long breath as he searched for anything that he could aim at before falling down the face of breaking surf and plunging underwater.

Swimming upward, this time he came up on the backside of a wave. His mind whirling, he caught a glimpse of Willoughby Spit, which was hundreds and hundreds of yards away. He treaded and turned, and, off in the distance, so far away, was Fort Wool. Somewhere behind it, more than a mile off, was Hampton.

Below the waves, he kept ordering himself to breathe like Namor, but the truth slowly settled in, causing him to feel dejected and hopeless. He'd tricked himself into believing the impossible. He couldn't inhale water. If he did, he'd choke. So he kept paddling upward, his slim arms getting heavy.

In time, it was torture to fight to the surface. Carter begged God to change him into Namor. He begged anything that would listen, including the big dark bundles of clouds that resembled blankets and bedding. He needed to be transformed like he'd never needed anything before.

But it didn't happen. He felt his ankle, and a wing didn't grow, while somewhere inside his neck, gills didn't form. He was just a regular kid about to drown in a hurricane. Frantic, he kept going. Past exhaustion and pain and fear and hurt, he swam, choking on the water and the wind and the rain, which seemed to clog his mouth when he tried to get a deep, raw swallow of air. Every so often, he'd get turned around and see the shoreline he'd left behind, but it kept getting farther away, so that he was scared he was going to die.

Hours seemed to pass, and his brain changed into a motor that drove his arms and legs. Maybe he was already dead. It was obvious he couldn't paddle through the storm and become the Boy Who Swam Across Hampton Roads. It was easier to quit than to keep working. He imagined drifting to the bottom like a boat with a hole in it. If he did, his arms wouldn't hurt, his brain wouldn't seem like a motor, and his lungs wouldn't beg.

A huge wave, larger than any yet, rose up blackly in the twilight. Its top exploded in white water as it started breaking and falling like a building losing a wall and tumbling toward the street. Tons of water plowed down on Carter, who was a speck, a useless little speck without any energy or will.

Deep under the surface, his side was hurting and everything was dark, dark green. He couldn't tell which way was up and barely cared. He drifted for a second or a minute or ten minutes. It was comfortable. He laughed a little and bubbles went from his mouth. He felt as brave as Edmund Hillary and Tenzing Norgay to be so calm. In a sudden rush of knowledge, he understood his dad's situation so much better, too. His father was swimming in a storm he couldn't control. A desire to live had nothing to do with living. The body could be weak and in pain, and the mind would be forced to surrender. There was absolutely no magic in the world.

He was an idiot to imagine himself something he

wasn't, to believe that wishes could change solid facts. Minnie was right, he didn't have any brains. Nothing. Nothing at all. His head was blank and dark and ridiculous.

Carter floated limply, crying. He sank deeper and prepared to suck water into his lungs, until, against his bare-naked back, something big brushed by, causing his quitting motor of a brain to spark and explode into a lunging wild-animal mind. He thought of the shark that he'd seen washed up on Willoughby Spit, and a burst of barely visible bubbles shot from his mouth. Desperate, he followed them, his rubbery arms pulling until he finally, weakly burst into the air between enormous swells. He breathed and cried and shouted for help. He was scared of getting eaten alive. That scared him to life, not to death.

So he swam furiously, even when his arms felt separate and useless. In the dark of night, lightning crackled overhead, but his mind was so feeble and beaten and deprived of oxygen and energy that he wasn't even scared of getting roasted. Black night enfolded him as though he were inside a tightly closed box. Time after time, he was forced down, and when he wasn't underwater, he was choking on salty foam and lashing surf.

Then a wave did something different. It washed him gently onto a hard, flat surface. Quick and grabby, Carter clawed till his hands caught on two jagged edges. The wave pulled out, but he stayed. When the next wave hit, the air was pounded from his lungs and his fingers got scraped, but he held on and got his legs, which were exhausted and accustomed to the motion of swimming, to push him upward. Slowly, holding firm, he dragged himself from the water and across a riprap of large, jagged stones.

In the darkness, Carter's fingers touched against slippery, matted grass. From there, he crawled through the pouring rain on hands and knees till his head tapped something hard. He felt at it, and it was so solid that he tucked his bare shoulders into the corner and, in a minute or less, fell asleep and dreamed of drowning in the heart-stopping darkness of Hampton Roads.

Chapter THIRTEEN

In the thick, gray drizzle of late morning, Carter stirred. Sitting up, his arms and legs felt flimsy and his head spun. He squinted into the misty, warm air before looking down at the emerald water surrounding him. Slowly, his eyes adjusted across the wide, rough channel, and, far away, he saw Willoughby Spit's smattering of homes on stilts, all of them smaller than Monopoly game pieces.

Carter felt the wall behind him and looked up at the strong bricks of Fort Wool, with its watchtower and deteriorating battlements that had been constructed around a hundred years before. He didn't wonder how he'd gotten there or consider it amazing. Instead, he staggered to his feet and circled the walled fortress so that he could look at the beautiful Chamberlain Hotel, which was large and impressive and less than a mile away, seated atop Old Point Comfort.

Carter tried to recollect why it had been important to him, which caused him to remember his dying father. He jerked about and gaped across the sweep of water separating him from home. Suddenly, he felt bleak and hopeless for having swum away as he had. He hadn't proved anything to anybody except to himself, and that was that people quit when they were too weak to live.

Facing out toward the Chesapeake Bay and the mouth of the Atlantic Ocean, he stumbled and sat down against a looming wall.

As a soft rain fell, hazy hours passed. Nothing was moving across the rough water except seagulls and two distant white boats, both of which battled their way along the shoreline of Willoughby Spit. Carter watched them as the rain came down, and eventually he nodded off, exhausted.

He woke to a voice. "Good God, he's here! He got here!"

"Liar!" somebody answered.

"He did! He's asleep!"

Feet crunched stone and a voice said, "Carter?"

Carter opened his eyes.

"Carter?"

"Yes, sir," he answered.

"Been looking for you all day. Nobody thought you could've survived. I mean, nobody."

Carter swallowed, his mouth dry. "What time is it?"

"Nearly time for dinner." The man adjusted the collar of his rain slicker, twisted about, and hollered, "Bring water!"

A moment later, another man stood in front of him. He shook his head and smiled. "How in the hell could he have come all this way?"

"I swam."

"God, kid, it's a miracle."

The man tried to wrap a blanket around him, but Carter wouldn't let him. "I'm sweaty," Carter said.

"Do you hurt anywhere?"

"Nothing's so bad."

The first man helped him drink from a canteen. The second man buckled a life jacket about him. Between them, they lifted Carter from the puddle and helped him walk to the boulders along the edge of the island. "We're gonna carry you down this riprap and get you into that dinghy that fella's trying to keep from bashing on the rocks. From there, if'n we don't flip, it's into that there coast guard cutter, and, if'n that don't flip, we're home."

"I can walk down," Carter told him.

The other man said, "Let him try. It's better than all three of us breaking our necks."

So Carter climbed down to the surging, violent water and somehow fell into the jostling dinghy, with its bow crunched and battered by the rocks. Behind Carter, one of the guys who'd rescued him tumbled and tore the pants of his slicker. Limping, the man waded into the rough waves and to the dinghy, which kept getting forced onto Fort Wool's stones. Slowly, with a motor that was barely effective, the four of them struggled out to the larger boat.

The pilot on the coast guard cutter shook his head. "Whew!" he hollered, and made a fist. "Amazing!"

A man cheerfully grabbed up the radio and called to shore. "This is Swydel. . . . Well, we got him! Kid was holed up on Fort Wool." The radio squawked back, and the man answered, "Yeah, it's incredible. It's downright out of this world."

A sailor laughed and said, "Carter, I've been on five of these missions, and you're the first person I ever found. Ever!"

"You're the Willoughby Spit Wonder," the pilot declared.

Carter looked at him distantly. "My dad. He's been sick. . . . He was dying when I left. Can you find out if he's alive?"

The radioman put the mouthpiece to his lips and said, "This is Swydel again. . . . Mr. Johnston wants to know about his dad. He's been sick. Can you give us his condition?"

Chapter
FOURTEEN

By the time she saw her son hunched on a bench in the coast guard's Willoughby Bay offices, Mrs. Johnston had experienced nearly every single emotion imaginable during the sixteen-hour period in which he'd been missing and found. Rushing across the room, her eyes were so red from tears that they resembled two permanently stained marbles, the whiteness gone forever. She slammed against him, wrapping her small arms tight about his body, and bawled loudly, her spirit aching with relief.

"Mom?" Carter said to her, his face crushed into the bosom of her blouse.

"Oh, Carter," she whimpered, patting down the hair on the back of his head.

"Mom?" he repeated, getting teary along with her.

"We thought you were lost. We thought you were gone."

On the way home, Mrs. Johnston kept reaching and touching him, tugging on his shirt and brushing a hand against his knees as if she weren't really sure he was there, as if she might be imagining he was beside her. "This is the happiest day of my life," she announced.

Uncomfortable, Carter studied the floor of the car. "Sorry" was all he could think to say, because he'd caused her so much grief.

"It's not your fault," she replied, jabbing a wadded tissue to her nose. "It's not your fault."

"It might've been."

"Minnie saw. Minnie saw you get pulled from off a sand dune. She said you couldn't do anything."

"She wasn't there."

"She was yelling to you."

Turning away, Carter stared at the storm damage along Ocean View Avenue. There were large and small pieces of shingles and decking on the side of the road. Telephone poles were tilted at odd angles, and water was everywhere, standing in ditches and drying in shallow lakes. As if Willoughby Spit had, for a short time, been at the bottom of the Chesapeake Bay, the road and streetcar tracks were completely covered with sand.

Carter told her, "I thought I saw someone on the beach. I . . . I didn't think it might be Minnie, though."

"It was, or we wouldn't have had any idea where you were." Mrs. Johnston slowed and directed the Henry J down their street, plowing through a patch of particularly deep sand.

Carter got out and stared along the block at a spot between homes, where the Owenses had once lived. Their house was missing as if it had never existed.

"It's strange, isn't it?" his mother said, rain covering her shoulders. "Thank goodness they got out."

"Is Papa Bear okay?"

"He's fine. Mr. Owens was mostly worried about you. He was very scared."

"He was?"

"All morning, even though his house was gone, he checked in."

Dazed, Carter noticed how his own home had lost about a hundred and fifty wooden shingles. Also, the pilings it rested atop were draped with sea grasses and nests of weeds and even old rope. In back, where steps had once been, there was a little shattered rowboat and a few dangling boards. He'd never seen anything like it.

Above, on the porch, the screen door creaked open and slammed shut, and Minnie emerged at the top of the stairs.

He studied her blank, unhappy look. "Hey."

"Hey, idiot."

Mrs. Johnston said, "Minnie, stop with the insults."

"I don't mind," Carter told her, humiliated that his sister knew what he'd done.

Mrs. Johnston said, "We should all be more grateful for each other. All of us."

Minnie came down the steps. For a second, it seemed as if she was going to hug her little brother. But she didn't. She knotted a fist and drilled him in the shoulder.

Carter stumbled backward, his whole body throbbing.

"Minnie, what has gotten into you?" her mother asked sharply, grabbing for her daughter's elbow.

"Him," she answered, stomping back up the steps.

Mrs. Johnston took a breath and loosened her rain bonnet. "She was worried you were gone. I think she felt guilty she didn't save you."

"She shouldn't have felt guilty at all."

Inside the house, Mrs. Johnston seated Carter on the couch. "Can I see Dad?" he asked.

"He's asleep," she answered before she went to warm a bowl of soup.

Minnie used the opportunity alone with her brother to say, "You're a cow penis."

Carter nodded.

"You almost killed yourself . . . and Mom and Dad, too."

"I . . . I was trying to help."

"How?"

"I was trying to show Dad about not quitting."

"You didn't help anything."

"I know."

"Do you get it now? You're not a stupid comic-book hero. You're just a dumb kid."

"I know."

"You can't fly, and you can't breathe underwater."

"I know."

Minnie's eyes furrowed with anger. "Stop agreeing with me and be normal."

"Okay."

"Talk back, or I'll snitch that you went into the water on purpose."

Faintly, he said, "Shut up, how about?"

"You shut up, you cow penis."

Their mother carried his soup into the room, and, while they waited for Mr. Johnston to awaken, Carter ate. "It's good," he told them.

Mrs. Johnston asked, "Did you swim all the way to Fort Wool?"

Softly, he answered, "I kind of washed up there. I guess I swam till I washed up."

"I thought maybe you'd held on to something. It seems . . . impossible. The waves were huge."

"I treaded water."

Mrs. Johnston twisted her dishtowel till it resembled a segmented rat's tail. Then she noticed and let it go slack. "The coast guard told us that they weren't likely to find your body. But your father knew different. He couldn't sleep till we got the word you were alive. That's the reason he's not up now."

Carter lowered his spoon. "On the boat, I was scared he might've died already."

"Last night, I thought he might." Mrs. Johnston draped the stretched dishtowel over a knee. "Did . . . did you think you were going to drown?"

"Not at first but pretty fast."

She nodded.

When it was dark outside and candles were lit because the electricity had been knocked out, Mrs. Johnston went to check on her husband. She called Carter up.

Cautiously, he climbed the stairs and entered the room. Hands in his pockets, he stood at the side of the bed.

Mr. Johnston's back was turned, so his wife called, "Carter's here and wants to see you."

"Namor," Mr. Johnston croaked, working to roll over. His face was yellow in the flickering light, but he smiled, which highlighted his swollen, puffy eyes and the gash on his forehead.

"I'm not Namor."

"You're right. You're not."

Mrs. Johnston slipped from the room, her skirt skimming the threshold like a bird slicing the air.

Mr. Johnston adjusted his hips, twisted, and put out a hand for his son to hold. "Wool Island?" he said.

"Yeah, that's where I got to."

"What are the chances?"

"Don't know."

"Like one in a million, I'd bet. If ever you want to believe in miracles, remember where you swam to. It's got to make you feel small."

"Maybe."

He kept his hand out for his son to hold and asked, "So, why? Why did you do it?"

Carter stared. "Did Minnie tell you I went on purpose?"

"She didn't have to."

He leaned forward. "Don't tell Mom."

"I won't." Mr. Johnston seemed so sad, though. "Tell me, Carter, did you think you were the Sub-Mariner or something?"

"A little."

Mr. Johnston swallowed. "When . . . when you asked me about that stuff . . . about your mom and Atlantis, I thought you were joking. I thought it wouldn't hurt anything if you thought it was true. I'm sorry."

Carter's shoulders lifted and dropped. "I . . . I went for other reasons, too."

"What were they?"

"They're stupid."

"I don't care. I want to know."

He hesitated. "I figured if I couldn't breathe water when I left, I could make it happen on the way. Have you thought if you want something bad enough, it'll happen?"

"Yes."

"It doesn't work."

Mr. Johnston wiped spittle from off his lip. "It

doesn't. I know." He coughed and snorted through his narrow nostrils. "If . . . if you'd died, Carter, I would've been eternally heartbroken and guilty. My ghost would've haunted the world in anguish."

Carter peered out the dark front windows toward the naval base, where distant lights twinkled in the otherwise pitch-black nighttime. He walked over and pressed his head against the screen, trying to see the sky. He couldn't, but he heard the rain falling. "Dad, it's the same way for me. I . . . I know you want us to be happy about it, but I don't ever want you to die, either. If you do, I'll be sad the same way. Did you know?"

Mr. Johnston cackled softly, a grin on his face. "Carter, sweetie, I think you've taken me wrong." He paused. "Carter, it's so dark. Come back."

Carter returned to the edge of the bed.

"I'd hate to think you'd be happy about my death. I don't want you to be. But what I've been trying to do is make it so that when I am gone, you're glad that I lived more than sad that I died. That's all."

"Maybe I won't be able to think that way."

"You'll be able." Mr. Johnston pointed at him

with a hand that rested palm-up on a pillow, like a flipped-over horseshoe crab. "You're a child. I'm an adult. That's the difference between what happened to you and what's happening to me. I've satisfied most of my dreams. In fact, you were one of them. It's not such a tragedy that I'll die now. But you, you're so young. You've got endless possibilities. You might change the world. Your loss is a loss to humanity, a loss of unknown talent and imagination, a loss of dreams."

Carter said, "If you go, that's how it would feel for me and Minnie and Mom."

Mr. Johnston touched the gash on his head. "I know. I see that. But . . . you need to tell me how I can help. Do you have any ideas?" Mr. Johnston rested silently, closing his eyes. In time, he opened them. "When you get lonely for me in the future, I want you to do something. Will you?"

"Maybe."

He grinned. "It's not hard, I promise. What I want is for you to think of the good times. Shut your eyes and imagine me and you and your mom and your sister laughing the way we have. Imagine every single detail, the smell, the scent, the light, and exactly how good it felt. We've had more fun than most other families put together."

Carter leaned against the bed. "It never seemed like you cared you were dying. To me, it always seemed like you were quitting."

Mr. Johnston snickered hoarsely. "I haven't ever quit, but I am dying. I can't stop it. I wish to holy heaven I could, but I can't."

Carter understood better than his father could guess. Sad and tired, he put his face down into the blankets and held it there till he was sure he wouldn't cry.

Chapter FIFTEEN

Somehow, from the brink of death, Ray Johnston improved, as he had before. Something, some unknown, impossible magic, kept his disintegrating body from quitting completely, and he was glad for the time, any time.

"Is Mom really at work?" Carter asked him, smiling.

Mr. Johnston tried to kick sand at his boy but couldn't manage it. "She's at work. If you don't believe it, you give her a call."

"Come on, Carter," Minnie said sharply.

"Bye, Dad."

"Bye," he told them, fidgeting like he could barely control his body anymore.

Minnie, Sylvia, and Carter cut down the beach, through the line of stones and dried seaweed to the edge of the water, where the cold surf swirled about their feet and the wind blew easily, fluttering their long-sleeved shirts.

They stopped in front of the amusement park, where workers had been refastening the roof onto the merry-go-round. It had blown off during the storm. After a minute, the three of them kept on, discussing nothing of importance and avoiding the worst news of all, that Sylvia's father wouldn't be coming home right away. He was being transferred to Berlin.

Far down the beach, Harrison's Pier stretched a few yards out into the water before disappearing in a thatch of poking pilings. A good portion of it had been swept out into the bay, and its broken remains resembled a set of rotten teeth. Anchored alongside what remained was a black barge with a pile driver that, during the day, thundered home new posts. In certain wind conditions, its sound could be heard clear to the tip of Willoughby Spit, where a different set of construction workers repaired the old ferry launch.

"The Sub-Mariner could pound those down with one fist."

"Actually, he couldn't. He doesn't exist," Minnie told him, "but imagine if they bolted your head to the pounder part. It'd be so fat and heavy the pilings would disappear into the sand."

He exhaled. "Why do you act so nasty?"

"Because most of the time you don't act smart. Figure it out! Comics are for kids. They aren't real books."

He put his hands in his pockets. "Well, what does wonderful Charlie like to read?"

She considered before answering. "I don't know."

"Probably girlie magazines."

Sylvia laughed.

Minnie said, "He probably only likes classics."

"Classic naked women."

Minnie confidently brushed her curly hair back. "I wouldn't talk, Carter. The Sub-Mariner wears skimpy swim trunks and no shirt."

"Charlie's bowlegged. Do you ever notice?"

Sylvia agreed. "Minnie, he sort of is."

Carter added, "It looks like he just got off a horse."

Shortly, the three of them passed up the bridge to Harrison's Pier and its restaurant and fishing store, both of which remained open during repairs. Minnie and Sylvia went to get two Cokes, and Carter checked to see if the new comics were out.

A few minutes later, he was in the restaurant, buying himself a jawbreaker. Secretly in love, he sat next to Sylvia instead of his sister. "Nothing came in, and they might not even carry superhero comics anymore."

Sylvia sighed. "Sorry."

"Guess I got to get them somewhere else now."

Minnie whispered, "Carter, did you see? Mr. Owens is right over there."

Carter turned around and spotted the old man, who was reading a book and sipping coffee. At his feet was Papa Bear, wide awake and looking anxious. "I think I should go say hi."

Carter got up and passed through the near-empty restaurant. "Hey, Mr. Owens."

He peeked up. "Carter, how are you?"

"Good. How's Papa Bear?"

"Fine. He'll be even better when the house is finished, but he's fine." Mr. Owens dug into a coat pocket and got his fingers on a square, brown clump that looked like dried mud. "He likes these. They're called Kix Dog Candy. That's why he's staring at me."

Carter smiled.

"How're your parents?" he asked.

Carter waited for Papa Bear to swallow his treat. "They're all right. Dad was in the hospital a few weeks ago, but he's back now."

The old man folded the page on his book and closed it. "Like I said, he's got nine lives, your father. If anyone ever wonders how you did the impossible and treaded water in a hurricane, all they've got to do is look at him."

"He's still not going to live. That's what doctors say."

"But he's living now?"

"Yes, sir."

"And your mother?"

"What?"

"How is she?"

"Still working at the shoe store."

"Is she okay, though?"

"Mostly." He thought a minute and said, "Maybe, since I got back, she smiles more. Dad teases that he wants her to get a new car, and she likes playing along. He says that our old car has seats that hurt his . . . you know . . . he says *ass*. Sorry."

"That's okay."

"But the seats don't bother Mom's butt, I guess."

Mr. Owens grinned. "Better to get a new one."

"That's what Dad tells her." Carter remembered his jawbreaker sitting over on the table. "Mr. Owens, I'll see you."

"See ya, Carter."

As Carter, Minnie, and Sylvia started for home, the sun hung like a shimmering yellow lantern over the shoreline of Hampton. Out on the Chesapeake, a ship slipped toward the Atlantic, its black stern cast in a blanket of golden light. Drifting overhead and beyond them, a flock of seagulls winged toward the point, barely flapping.

Carter watched them, then he took his jawbreaker out of his mouth. "Wish I could fly. I really do."

Minnie, who was a few steps ahead, turned around. "Do you ever stop wishing?"

"No."

"Well then, you ought to wish for better grades."

"I don't want to waste wishes. When I get one, I want it to be really good."

"Me, too," Sylvia agreed.

Carter looked at both of them, his lonely eyes reflecting the sun. "Minnie, if you don't wish big, you shouldn't wish at all."

OTHER BOOKS BY JONATHON SCOTT FUQUA

The Reappearance of Sam Webber

WINNER OF THE AMERICAN LIBRARY ASSOCIATION ALEX AWARD

A *Booklist* EDITORS' CHOICE

A *School Library Journal* BEST BOOK OF THE YEAR

"A white eleven-year-old becomes fast friends with a black
janitor and learns about racism, loss, grief, forgiveness,
and the landscape of Baltimore in this heartfelt . . . debut."
—*Publishers Weekly*

"Addresses prejudice and overcoming urban fears . . .
a realistic picture of the trials in a single-parent family . . .
Highly recommended."   —*Library Journal*

Darby

A BOOK SENSE 76 TOP TEN PICK

AN OPPENHEIM TOY PORTFOLIO PLATINUM AWARD WINNER

AN INTERNATIONAL READING ASSOCIATION
NOTABLE CHILDREN'S BOOK

"Darby's first-person narrative is frank and immediate without
being cute, expressing what it's like for an ordinary white kid
who suddenly discovers evil—and courage—where she lives."
—*Booklist*

"The root of this work stems from a series of oral history
interviews the author conducted—and that's what makes it
ring with truth. Darby symbolizes how one person, even
a child, can make a difference."   —*Kirkus Reviews*

JONATHON SCOTT FUQUA

is the author of many acclaimed books for young readers, including *Darby*, a *Book Sense 76* Top Ten Pick, an Oppenheim Toy Portfolio Platinum Award Winner, and an IRA Notable Children's Book. His debut novel, *The Reappearance of Sam Webber*, won an ALA 2000 Alex Award and was a *School Library Journal* Best Book of the Year.